To Grace an

with best wishes

Stuart

Stuart R McRorie was born in 1948 in the Worcestershire village of Ombersley, and has lived in the county ever since.

He attended Queen Elizabeth I grammar school Hartlebury.

After leaving school he worked in many different jobs, including metrology engineer, estates manager and landscape gardener.

He is now retired, and he now loves nothing more than to spend his spare time on his allotment, growing prize winning sweet-peas and a wide variety of organic vegetables. He enjoys playing chess at the local drop-in chess club, in Bewdley, where he has lived with his wife for over thirty years.

He always harboured an ambition to write, but only came to do so when he was recovering from a serious illness in 2014. Having taken so long to write his first novel he is now working on his second.

To Elaine

This could never have happened without you

Stuart R McRorie

THE SYTCHFORD SPY

AUSTIN MACAULEY PUBLISHERS™

LONDON • CAMBRIDGE • NEW YORK • SHARJAH

Copyright © Stuart R McRorie (2020)

The right of Stuart R McRorie to be identified as author of this work has been asserted by him in accordance with section 77 and 78 of the Copyright, Designs and Patents Act 1988.

All rights reserved. No part of this publication may be reproduced, stored in a retrieval system, or transmitted in any form or by any means, electronic, mechanical, photocopying, recording, or otherwise, without the prior permission of the publishers.

Any person who commits any unauthorised act in relation to this publication may be liable to criminal prosecution and civil claims for damages.

This is a work of fiction. Names, characters, businesses, places, events, locales, and incidents are either the products of the author's imagination or used in a fictitious manner. Any resemblance to actual persons, living or dead, or actual events is purely coincidental.

A CIP catalogue record for this title is available from the British Library.

ISBN 9781528980814 (Paperback)
ISBN 9781528980838 (ePub e-book)

www.austinmacauley.com

First Published (2020)
Austin Macauley Publishers Ltd
25 Canada Square
Canary Wharf
London
E14 5LQ

Thanks to Derek Beattie for his book, *The Home Front in Ludlow in the Second World War.* And to Bewdley and Stourport libraries for their all their reference material and resources.

Chapter 1

One unusually hot afternoon in the spring of 1944 a brightly painted Gypsy caravan rumbled along an otherwise deserted road close by the River Teme in Worcestershire.

On either side lay hop fields and orchards where sheep grazed beneath the trees and lambs suckled greedily; their tails quivering with delight. The air was filled with the sweet scent of early hawthorn blossom and the buzzing of countless bees that were drawn to it.

The caravan was being pulled by Nelson, a brown and white piebald horse. A couple of brown hens slept in a wooden crate tied to the side of the caravan, and a canary sang from its perch in a cage that swung gently under the overhanging canvas that sheltered the doorway. A white nanny goat trotted behind the caravan tethered by a fraying length of rope.

A suntanned old man and a black-haired young girl walked on either side of the horse, talking to one another across the animal's lowered neck, as it strained to haul the heavy wagon.

The girl held a tattered black umbrella above her head for shade. The faded blue dress she wore matched the sky where a thin veil of high clouds was forming.

"Why is there a war going on?"

"Why can't everywhere be like this----always?" the girl asked herself as she looked around her.

A sharp pain in her foot drove these questions from her mind as she slipped off her boot and shook out a tiny pebble that had somehow found its way in.

"How much further is it, Granddad?" asked Florence Lovesmith for the third time that afternoon.

"Near three or four miles, I reckon. Should only take us a couple of hours to get there, if we keep ploddin' on steady," replied the old man as he fanned himself with a battered trilby hat. He wore a collarless shirt with the sleeves rolled up to the elbows and corduroy trousers supported by red braces. He had on his feet stout boots made for walking the roads. Although every item of his dusty clothing was showing signs of wear, and he was in need of a shave, he nevertheless in no way seemed downtrodden. As he walked, he looked around as though he was the lord of the manor surveying his estate.

"See there. That's the church steeple. Won't be long now," he eventually said, pointing to where the spire showed above the treetops.

"Good. I'm exhausted. Even Prince looks weary," said the girl, looking down to where a rangy mongrel dog padded in the horse's shadow, panting in the heat.

They fell silent as Florence wondered what she might find when they arrived in Sytchford. Her grandparents had told her a lot about the place, but she had never been there before.

The hop fields and orchards of Kent were where she had grown up amongst her family and friends. They had moved around, never staying in one place too long, but never far from the south coast of England. That was where Florence felt at home, and she hadn't wanted to leave, but her mother insisted that she should spend the summer with her grandparents.

"They're not as young as they were. They need a bit of help and you're old enough now to make the journey on your own," she said.

Florence argued and pleaded to stay, but she had no say in the matter. Her mother had made up her mind, and so she was packed off one morning on the long and arduous train journey to Worcester

It was a daunting journey for the eleven-year-old girl to make all alone. The train was packed with servicemen and servicewomen, and there were frequent stops along the way. No one knew when they would eventually reach their destination, but this being wartime, there were few complaints.

Florence was lucky to have found a seat when she got on the train, but soon after it set off, she gave it up to a soldier on crutches and spent the rest of the journey standing in the corridor.

By the time the train finally arrived, several hours behind schedule, Florence was exhausted and afraid that there would be no one to meet her. To her immense relief, she spotted her grandmother straight away and ran to meet her.

Since then, for three days, they had made their way slowly along the road to Sytchford, and Florence was beginning to come to terms with the situation she found herself in.

She had not seen her grandparents for several years, but right from the moment her Gran had thrown her arms around her on the station platform, she knew that she was loved. Now she was beginning to look forward to being with them for the summer.

Gran was a small, weather-beaten woman with twinkling dark eyes. Her hair had remained jet black, though, usually covered by a either a wide-brimmed hat or a brightly coloured headscarf. She wore gold earrings and smoked a clay pipe with a long-curved stem. She had quite a reputation as a fortune teller, and as they travelled slowly through the countryside, Florence listened and learned as the elderly Gypsy passed on what she had learned from her own grandmother when she was a child.

This afternoon, while Florence and Granddad where walking, Gran rested inside the caravan. As the road was smooth and level, Nelson was judged able to cope with the added load.

All day long, the heat had been steadily building up and ahead, a huge thundercloud was beginning to take shape. The snow-white head billowed upwards while far below, its flat, black base cast a shadow that moved slowly across the land. It reminded Florence of the great trees she had seen standing in rolling parkland on her train journey. The illusion dissolved as a flicker of lightening lit up the cloud from within and seconds later the air trembled, and she heard the ominous rumble of thunder. Her head felt strange. It was as though she was being crushed by a great invisible weight. She had a sudden feeling of foreboding. Something – she didn't know what – was about to happen.

Her granddad walked along the roadside verge, making the most of what shade there was close to the tall hedgerow.

"Not far to go now, Nelson," he said softly as he gave the tired animal a hearty pat on the neck, sending a cloud of dust into the air.

The road ahead was empty due to petrol rationing, which had put a stop to all but essential journeys for most people. The only sounds were the steady clip-clop of Nelson's hooves, the rumble of the wagon wheels, and the twittering of the canary.

Still, Florence was uneasy.

Half a mile behind the caravan, a red open-topped sports car was travelling on the same road towards Sytchford. The driver was hoping to impress the attractive redhead in the passenger seat, and the distance between them and the caravan was rapidly shrinking.

"Slowdown, will you, Robert?" the girl said as the wind tugged at her headscarf.

"Looks like rain. Don't want to get caught in it do you, Claire?" answered the young airman.

"Why don't we stop and put the hood up?"

"We'll be alright if I step on it," he replied confidently.

This was his favourite stretch of road: a series of tight bends followed by a mile-long straight stretch where he could push the car to its limit. A race against the oncoming storm was just the excuse he needed.

He accelerated out of the final bend expecting the road ahead to be clear and was surprised and annoyed to find a goat and a gypsy caravan directly in his path. There was nothing coming in the other direction so he pressed his foot down to the floor and drove on.

Claire shut her eyes as Robert pulled out and with an angry blast of the horn, overtook, sending clouds of dust swirling around the startled travellers and creating chaos as Nelson reared in fright.

"MANIAC!" shouted Florence, as the car hurtled past.

She turned to see Granddad climbing to his feet from the roadside ditch.

"I'm alright, don't fuss," he said as he dusted himself down. "Nelson took fright and caught me off balance."

He patted the frightened animal and spoke to it softly as he checked to see if it had been in any way hurt.

"That driver will end up killing someone!" said Gran as she climbed down from the caravan. "I'd like to get my 'ands on 'im!"

As she spoke, big spots of rain began to fall.

"Quick. Let's get inside," said Florence.

"Anyway, serves 'im right! E's in for a proper soakin!" said Granddad when they were safely inside.

His words were nearly drowned out by a huge clap of thunder and next moment, the heavens opened.

"Right, let's put the kettle on," suggested Gran as she lit the small cooking stove. They soon sat sipping their tea, watching the lightning flicker across the black sky and the rain turning the road into a river.

Half an hour later, the storm passed, and the sun broke through. The dog emerged from the hedgerow and shook itself vigorously, sending showers of water into the air. Steam began to rise from the tarmac and from Nelson's back as the travellers resumed their journey, refreshed by the rain and mugs of tea.

Robert Westwood's journey was proving to be altogether less pleasant. He had eventually pulled over to the side of the road and hastily put the hood up, but not before both he and his passenger had been drenched. Then just to make matters worse the car refused to start until the battery was almost run down, and even then, the engine spluttered and misfired so badly that they could only crawl along at walking speed.

Claire sat fuming in stony silence until they finally stopped outside a garage in the centre of the village.

"Look. I'm sorry. I thought we could make it before the –" Robert began.

"I don't want to hear it," Claire interrupted as she got out of the car. "That's *so* typical. You always think you know best. Well, that's the final straw. I've had enough. We're finished!"

And with that, she slammed the car door shut, strode across the street and disappeared into a large redbrick house, leaving Robert sitting in his soaking wet seat, holding his head in his hands.

Later that day, as the shadows lengthened and the air grew cool, the caravan crossed the bridge over the River Teme and entered Sytchford's main street.

Over centuries, Sytchford had grown from a small hamlet into a substantial village. It occupied a spot where the little Sytch brook joined the River Teme. From the bridge, the high street led towards a crossroads, where a war memorial stood: a simple stone cross beneath which were chiselled names of those who had died in the previous war. The village was large enough to support an assortment of shops that supplied the inhabitants with most of what they needed. These were scattered randomly along the main street between the houses. The caravan passed by a butcher's, an ironmonger's, a baker's and a post office, amongst others. Most of the shops were modest in size; often little more than a converted front room in someone's home.

One shop stood out from the rest. It had two large windows, one on either side of the doorway. The door had a glass panel on which the words 'Evans' Grocery Store' were displayed.

The shops shared the thoroughfare with an odd assortment of houses. Some were handsome redbrick Georgian buildings, and others were older timber-framed structures, warped and crooked through age. Big houses sat next to small ones, and alleyways in-between gave glimpses of the gardens behind where wallflowers and forget-me-nots would soon give way to the early summer blooms of lupins, sweet peas and larkspur.

Apart from the Lovesmith's caravan, the street seemed deserted and Florence wondered if everyone was hiding behind their net curtains. Then from nowhere, a black cat shot across the road in front of them and dashed down an alleyway.

Florence and her granddad exchanged meaningful looks as they carried on to the crossroads, where Sytchford's garage and filling station stood. The garage was a large wooden building, with a corrugated iron roof. There was a single petrol pump on the forecourt, and above the shed's double doors the words 'Tolley's Automobile Repairs' were painted in red lettering.

As they passed by, a man in blue overalls was just shutting the double doors, and they caught a glimpse of the red sports car with its bonnet raised and a toolbox lying nearby with spanners scattered around.

"Looks like 'e's got a problem," observed Granddad.

"Good. Serves 'im right!" exclaimed Florence.

Across from the garage, on the opposite corner, Florence became aware of two children watching from the pavement. The boy was about her own age, with ginger hair, similar to the girl's, except his was short and curly while hers was tamed, being woven into two long plaits. She was perhaps just a year younger than Florence, and she was wearing round glasses with thin metal frames.

Ash Sinton and his sister Violet lived with their older sister and their mother in Orchard House. They had lived all their lives in the village, where they knew everyone, and everyone knew them. Any new arrival was an event, and they were determined not to miss a thing as they stood watching the caravan go by. They were normally well-mannered children, but they were so engrossed by the colourful caravan, and the young suntanned girl, with short, jet black hair, that they were staring quite rudely when Florence stopped and demanded, "What are you two starin' at? Never seen Gypsies before?"

Ash and Violet looked at each other for a moment, lost for words, and then Violet stammered, "Er, sorry, we were just... er... just... looking."

"There's no *law* against looking," said Ash.

Gemini and Aries, thought Florence.

"You live 'ere?" she asked.

"Yes," replied Ash, "this is our house." He pointed to the large redbrick building behind him.

15

"Come on, Florence," called Granddad. She turned and continued her journey leaving Ash and Violet still standing and watching as they moved on.

"The Gypsies have arrived," announced Ash, when they finally went inside.

"Oh, have they? I thought they'd be here soon," replied their mother. "And where have you two been till now?"

"Nowhere really. Just in the street," replied Ash

"Well, now that you're back, you can go and see to the geese and hens for me. Then you can have some supper and listen to the radio for half an hour before bed."

Later, as the children climbed the stairs, their mother called after them, "Don't forget your prayers and remember to say a prayer for your father."

"Yes, we will," they both answered. Then violet asked, "When do you think Dad will come back?"

It was a question that she asked frequently, and it was a question that her mother could not give a truthful answer to. Their father, Sidney Sinton, had been reported 'Missing in Action' during the allied invasion of Sicily last August. She didn't know *if* he would return, let alone when.

"One day. Soon, I hope," was the best she could say.

"Go on up to bed now and straight to sleep."

Ash was not sleepy though.

"Let's go down by the river tomorrow. We can have a look at the Gypsy camp on the way," he whispered.

"Mom says we're not to talk to them. We're to keep away," replied Violet.

Meanwhile, the Lovesmiths had continued on, over the crossroads, until they came to the far side of the village, where they stopped on a patch of rough ground between the black-smith's home and the brook.

A figure appeared at the smithy's doorway. He was short but wide across the shoulders with muscular arms. He was almost completely bald, except for a few tufts of hair that formed a semi-circle round the back of his head, and bushy sideburns that covered most of his round face. He came rolling towards the caravan with a wide grin, which revealed gaps between a few teeth with gold fillings.

"Aha! I knew you'd be here today, I did so!" he exclaimed. "Good to see you again! Can't believe it's been almost a year. Don't know where the time goes."

"And who have we here?" he asked.

"This is my granddaughter Florence. Come to stay with us for a while," said Gran proudly.

"Ah. I can see the likeness, I can so!"

"Some young fool in a sports car nearly ran us off the road earlier. I ended up in the ditch," said Granddad.

"Red sports car was it, by any chance?"

"It was. Do you know 'oose it is?"

"Only one round these parts. Belongs to Major Westwood's lad. He be a rare one and no mistake. I could tell you a few tales about young Robert. Oh yes! But that'll keep for now. You'll be a wantin' to get fire lit. Dare say you'm all tired and hungry. You know where the tap is. I'll just be off to look into the Crystal Ball for a bit."

"Are you a fortune-teller?" asked Florence eagerly.

"Lord! No," the blacksmith laughed. "Crystal Ball's the name of the village pub." With that, Alf Carter ambled off to quench his thirst.

"Thirsty work, bein' a blacksmith," observed Granddad as he unharnessed Nelson.

"Thirsty work, towin' a caravan," replied Gran. "Fetch Nelson some water. Poor thing must be parched."

Later, as the family sat round the campfire, Florence slipped off her boots and took out a worn piece of cardboard from each. She poked a finger through a hole in the sole of one of the boots. It had definitely grown bigger during the day.

"Look at that Gran," she said.

"Don't you fret my lovely. We'll get them fixed tomorrow. There's a good cobbler in the village," said Gran, seeing what a state the boots were in.

"Fancy sending the poor mite off without a decent pair of boots on 'er feet," the old lady thought angrily.

Just then, a man came cycling along the road. He stopped and came marching over. He was tall and thin, and his face was made to look even thinner by his large ears, which stuck out beneath a helmet with the letter 'W' on the front. A cigarette stub dangled from his lower lip. He had on a uniform that seemed rather too big for him.

He didn't stop to introduce himself but straight away, began barking out instructions.

"You'll have to put that fire out! There's a war on, you know and blackout regulations state quite clearly that all forms of light must be h'extinguished during the hours of darkness, and that includes your campfire. So get it put out, h'as of now!"

Somehow, the cigarette stayed in place while he was speaking. The red end bobbing up and down as his thin lips moved.

"Are you serious? Nobody's goin' to see this little fire from thousands of feet up there. 'Ow we supposed to cook a meal without a fire?" demanded Granddad.

"That's not my problem," replied the warden. "I'll 'ave to report you if you don't put it out. Look. I'll be back in h'arf an 'our. See that its h'extinguished by then," he muttered as he turned and remounted his bike.

"That was Albert Skinner, wasn't it?" asked Granddad as the Air Raid Warden cycled away into the gathering darkness. "Shame they can't find 'im summat useful to do instead of pesterin' folk for no good reason."

"I suppose he's just doin' 'is job. You never know when there might be an air raid," replied Gran.

"What? Out 'ere? I shouldn't think so! Anyway, 'e didn't ave to be so rude about it."

"I think it's just is nature. 'E don't know any better. Anyway, we'd best do as 'e says. We're all about ready for bed I reckon," said Gran.

Granddad was right. There was no air raid over Sytchford that night, and the Lovesmiths and Sintons slept soundly as the foxes prowled around the hencoops, and the owls hunted for mice in the barns and farmyards.

Chapter 2

Next morning, Ash and Violet were out early. The sun was once again shining brightly, burning off the mist from the river valley.

"Don't go by the Gypsy camp," their mother warned as they hurried through the back door.

"We won't, Mom. Promise," shouted Violet as they headed down the path.

"And don't go falling in the brook again either," their mother replied, but they were already out of earshot.

The path led through the orchard, over fields, passing close by the smithy. They could see the caravan parked on the rough patch of ground with a tent nearby. No one seemed to be around; just the white goat tethered to a stake in the ground. Ash was tempted to take a closer look, but Violet was having none of it.

"We promised," she said.

"You promised. I didn't," Ash reminded her.

"Come on. Don't be such a pest. Let's go down by the brook."

They followed a rough cart track leading between the fields and then cut across a meadow to reach one of their favourite spots. At a bend in the brook, generations of thirsty cattle had waded into the water wearing away the bank and creating a wide, deep pool. There was a big ash tree on the bank. Its smooth trunk stood straight and clean, until 10 feet up, where a strong branch reached out over the water. From this branch hung a rope with an old tyre tied to it. Most of the village children had gone home soaked to the skin at one time or another after playing on the rope swing.

Violet didn't feel like playing though just then, and she decided to sit quietly on a log and watch her brother swinging backwards and forwards over the water. Her thoughts turned to when they had come here two years ago. Their father had been on leave for two weeks and they had taken a picnic to that very spot and had such a happy time playing on the swing, catching sticklebacks with their little fishing nets and paddling in the brook. Their father had taken photographs. It all seemed so long ago now, but at least they had the photos to remind them.

Her thoughts were interrupted by a loud '*Plop*' as a water vole dived into the brook almost under her feet. She watched as it swam across to the far bank sending ripples outwards over the surface of the water. It climbed out and shook the water from itself before disappearing into a hole just above the waterline. There was something so comical about the furry little creature that she could not help but smile.

Ash soon grew tired of the swing and wondered what to do next.

"Let's go and have a look in the old barn. See if the barn owl's in there," he said.

"How are we going to get across the brook?" Violet asked. "It's too deep to wade across."

The Sytch brook was not very wide but the recent storm had brought the water level up, and the current was flowing strongly. Ash, however, was not to be deterred.

"I know where we can cross," he said as he set off downstream. Violet followed reluctantly. Before long, they came to a fallen willow tree that bridged the brook. Its roots still clung to the bank and tangled branches still carried fresh leaves.

The children made their way carefully over the slippery tree trunk, working their way through the branches that stuck out at all angles.

"What have you done to your knee? It's bleeding," Ash said when they jumped down onto the far bank.

"Scraped it on something. It'll be alright."

"Don't get blood on your sock. Mom will *kill* you," she warned.

20

Violet wiped the blood away with a dock leaf, and they ran across the meadow, watched by a few sheep and lambs that were lying in the shade of an elm tree.

The barn was in the far corner of the field close by a gate in the overgrown hedge. On the other side of the hedge, a narrow winding lane led back towards the village.

When they reached the barn, they found the huge doors padlocked.

"Come on then. Let's go back along the lane," said Violet. She was secretly quite glad that the barn was locked. She sensed trouble ahead.

"Let's have a look round first. There might be another way in," Ash insisted as he led the way along the side of the barn. A few sheep were lying under the shade of the hedge, and they jumped up as he came round the corner and ran off to join the rest of the flock under the elm tree.

He soon found what he was looking for. Two planks had slipped down leaving a long, narrow gap in the wall.

"Come on, we can get through here," he urged, but Violet hung back, reluctantly.

"I don't think we should," she said.

"Well, I'm going in even if you aren't," he answered as he pushed his head and shoulders through the gap. Moments later, he had pulled himself through into the barn.

At first, all he could see was dust floating in the shafts of sunlight that shone through gaps in the shell of the neglected building, but as his eyes adjusted to the shadows, he began to make out more.

Hay was scattered on the floor around an old wagon that had collapsed onto its side: the broken wheel propped against a wall.

He looked around and spotted the barn owl sitting high above on a massive oak crossbeam.

"Can you see anything?" Violet asked, as she poked her head through the gap.

"Yes. Come on," he whispered.

Violet knew it was the wrong thing to do and she was making a bad choice, but she really wanted to see the barn owl, and moments later, she found herself standing next to her brother looking up at the white owl. She was lost for words, and even Ash was silent for once. Time seemed to stand still as the children and the owl looked at each other, then the spell was broken as they heard a car approaching.

They stood frozen to the spot hoping it would drive past, but instead, it stopped right beside the barn and they heard the gate open on its rusty hinges. Someone was coming.

"Quick, let's go!" urged Ash.

"It's too late," replied Violet. "Get under here."

They ducked down behind the hay wagon and pulled some dusty sacking over them as the doors swung open and the barn was flooded with light. The barn owl flew out and made for the cover of a nearby oak tree.

As Violet and Ash lay behind the wagon, they could hear someone moving about, and once or twice, the footsteps came right up to their hiding place. They held their breath and waited to be discovered.

After what seemed like hours, they heard the barn doors swing shut and the padlock rattle as it was locked. The vehicle drove off soon afterwards, leaving a cloud of smoke hanging in the air.

"That was a close thing," said Ash, brushing himself down. "Did you see who it was?"

"No. How could I? I'm never going to listen to your stupid ideas again. We're covered in dirt and probably got spiders in our hair and everywhere. What if we'd been caught?" she replied angrily.

"Well, we weren't caught, were we?"

"Look over there," he said, spotting something in the far corner.

"Let's just get out of here. I want to go home!" Violet said, but Ash was already uncovering a stack of cardboard boxes hidden under a dustsheet.

"It's tinned stuff: corned beef, pears, sausages. Look, there's tons of it."

Violet went over to see for herself. She picked up a can and took it to where the light was better.

"Look at this one. Peaches. Mrs Evans hasn't been able to get tinned peaches since… I don't know, years probably."

"What's it all doin' here?" Ash asked.

"How should I know? Come on. Let's go, before they come back," Violet answered.

They clambered out into the daylight and hurried home by way of the lane, feeling as though they were being watched.

When peace returned to the meadow, the barn owl flew back to the old barn and settled down to wait for nightfall.

Meanwhile, Florence and her gran were going into the village. Apart from getting Florence's boots fixed, they needed to register with the shopkeepers so that they could get ration books, without which they would not be allowed to buy most of the things they needed: butter, cheese, sugar, soap. The list was getting longer and longer as the war dragged on. Everything was scarce.

They knew it would be a long process and didn't expect to get back to the caravan till late afternoon. What with having to answer the same questions and showing the same identity papers in each and every shop.

They were passing the garage as the red sports car was about to pull out onto the road. Gran stopped, blocking the way.

The driver gave two loud blasts of the horn.

Gran and Florence held their ground.

The driver gave another longer blast of the horn.

"What do you think you're doing? Move. I'm in a hurry," he shouted.

People stopped and looked.

"Seems you're always in an 'urry. Too much of an 'urry if you ask me," Gran replied.

"I've got important business to see to, and you've no right to block the road. **Now get out of the way!**"

"You nearly had our vardo in the ditch yesterday, and my 'usband's lucky 'is ribs 'ent broke. People like you oughtn't to be allowed on the road!" Gran replied angrily.

"Ah. You're those Gypsies, are you? Well, you're lucky you didn't *all* end up in the ditch. Where you belong!"

With that, he accelerated out of the garage and swerved around them onto the road, speeding recklessly away towards the bridge.

"I'm reporting you to the police!" Gran shouted after the car, but her words were drowned out by the roar of the car's engine.

"I say, are you all right?"

Florence turned to see a white-haired, elderly man wearing a black shirt with a white clerical collar.

"Well yes, we're fine. Thank you," Gran replied. "But that's no thanks to that fool." She then proceeded to tell him all about their encounter the previous day.

"I'm afraid that young man *is* becoming something of a nuisance. I've been meaning to have a word with his father. Anyway, I hope you won't have any more trouble. This is usually a quiet little town. I'm Clifton Wren, by the way. Vicar of St Christopher's," he continued.

Florence had been fascinated by something the vicar was carrying on a strap over his shoulder. The brown leather case could have contained a gas mask, only it looked too small and too expensive.

"S'cuse me. Is that some sort of gas mask?" she asked.

"Oh, these are my binoculars. I'm something of an amateur ornithologist. A bird watcher, you know," he added, seeing Florence's puzzled expression. "I'm just on my way to the woods to see if the pied flycatchers have returned yet. Tiny birds. They come here every year, you know. Travel thousands of miles. Migrants, you see. They come from somewhere in Africa, probably. No one knows for sure. Yes, mm, fascinating. Well, I mustn't keep you. Glad there's no harm done. Goodbye. Nice to have met you."

"'Es goin' to watch a bird?" Florence whispered as the vicar walked away.

"That's what 'e said," replied Gran.

Florence pondered this strange behaviour. It had never occurred to her that watching birds would be something that a grown man would set out to do.

"What's a pied flycatcher look like, Gran?" she asked.

"I don't know," she replied. "But I know what a wren looks like," she chuckled as the vicar disappeared round a corner.

"There's the cobbler's, look, just over there. We'll go there first," she said pointing to a little black and white building wedged in between two larger redbrick houses.

They stepped inside the shop to be greeted by an overpowering smell of pipe tobacco and old shoe leather. As Florence's eyes adjusted to the dim light, she saw boots and shoes piled up everywhere. The elderly cobbler sat at a bench facing the window, which seemed to be the only source of light. He was busy hammering nails into an upturned boot. He held the nails in a row between his teeth, and it was only when he had removed the last one and hammered it in place that he turned to look at the visitors. His face was divided in two by an enormous moustache, which curled up at the ends, and a pair of half-moon spectacles that somehow balanced on the tip of his nose.

"What can I do for you, ladies?" he enquired cheerfully.

"It's Florence's boots. Worn right through. I'm 'opin' you'll be able to fix 'em for us," replied Gran.

"Let's have a look at 'em, shall we?"

Florence removed the boots from her feet and handed them to the cobbler who gave them a quick inspection before saying, "I can put new soles and heels on. The uppers are still sound. Come back and pick them up next Saturday. It'll cost you five shillings mind."

"Oh. Don't suppose there's any way you could fix 'em today? Only she 'asn't got another pair," pleaded Gran.

"Look. See all these?" he answered, gesturing towards the mounds of footwear. "They all need doing, and nobody wants to wait. If I was to do yours first, there'd be hell to pay.

"I'll have a look out the back. I think I can find another pair that'll fit," he sighed on seeing the disappointment on Florence's face.

"Wait here a minute," he said as he went into the back room. When he returned, he was holding a pair of shiny black shoes, which were unlike any she had owned before. Instead of laces, these were fastened by a strap. When she held them, they seemed to weigh almost nothing. She tried them on.

"Not very practical," sniffed Gran.

"They fit perfect," said Florence.

"How much are they?" asked Gran.

"Good quality. I know who owned 'em and they've been well looked after as you can see. You can have 'em for a pound."

"Ten shillin's," replied Gran.

"Fifteen, and you've got a pair of shoes and a pair of boots as good as new for a pound."

"Done!" said Gran shaking the cobbler's hand. "Is it alright if we give you 'alf now and the rest next week?"

Chapter 3

Ash and Violet were both famished when they eventually got home from the barn.

"What's for lunch, Mom?" Ash asked.

"You can have poached egg on toast once you've washed your hands properly," their mother replied. "When you've finished, I want you to do some shopping for me. I've written you a list, but I don't expect you'll be able to get everything. Just do your best."

So, as soon as they had finished eating, they set off for the high street.

They had a few different shops to visit, but it did not take them long, and they were just leaving the butcher's when something happened that would alter the rest of their summer.

"Shall we go and see if there's anyone on the allotments?" Ash suggested.

"You go. I'll take the shopping home and get on with my painting," replied Violet as she dropped the change into her purse.

"Alright then, but –" he stopped in mid-sentence. "Careful, you've just dropped a sixpence." He pointed to the pavement where the small silver coin was rolling toward a group of bigger boys. One of them spotted it and swooped on it before Ash or Violet had a chance.

"Hey, that's ours," exclaimed Ash.

"Not now it ain't," replied the boy.

Ash knew who they were. Nodder Crump, Billy Butcher and Jack Spragg. All troublemakers who liked to push their weight around when they were in a gang.

Violet stood in front of Nodder, with her hands on her hips. She only came up to his chest, but she wasn't about to let him get away with her mother's change if she could help it. "That's stealing, that is. Give it back," she said as firmly as she could.

"Finders keepers, losers weepers. Innit?" he replied, and his friends laughed mockingly.

Ash tried to grab the coin from him as he held it out, but he just raised his arm so that it was out of reach. Billy Butcher pushed Ash in the chest and glared at him threateningly, as he staggered backwards.

Florence and her gran were on their way back from the shops just then and saw what was happening. Florence hurried up to the gang and confronted them.

"That belongs to 'er," she said pointing to Violet. "Give it back."

"What's it got to do with you?" demanded Jack Spragg.

"Give it back! It isn't yours!"

"Make me," challenged Nodder.

"Do as she says. You've 'ad your fun," said Gran as she caught up with her granddaughter.

The three boys reluctantly gave way. They had no intention of getting on the wrong side of Granny Lovesmith. That could bring about bad luck.

The boy held out his hand and Violet took back the sixpence, and the three lads swaggered off, pushing and shoving one another as they went.

"Thank you," said Violet.

"S'alright. No problem. I don't like bullies," said Florence.

"What's your name?" asked Ash.

"Florence. What's yours?"

"I'm Ashford Sinton. Everybody calls me Ash."

"And I'm his sister, Violet."

"Well, we're pleased to meet you both," said Gran. "Can't stop I'm afraid. We've a lot to do, but you mind 'ow you go now."

"We will. Thanks again," said Violet.

They hurried home, keeping a wary eye out for trouble for the second time that day.

"Those are the kids from Orchard House," Gran mused as they made their way back to the caravan. "Ash and Violet. 'Er's well named."

"Why d'you say that?"

"Well, the way she stood up to them lads put me in mind of violets. They're delicate little things to look at, violets, but they're brave and tough as those old boots of yours really," she chuckled.

"Somethin' tells me we're goin' to see a lot more of those two," she added thoughtfully.

"Did you manage to get everything?" Violet's mother asked when the children got back home.

"Nearly," replied Violet. "There wasn't any sugar, but Mrs Evans said they should have some in by Tuesday."

"We'll have to be careful not to use very much. I think there's just about enough," her mother said as she peered inside a large enamel container. "Where's the change then?" she enquired, holding her hand out.

Violet produced her purse from a pocket and emptied it out into the waiting hand.

Her mother did some rapid mental arithmetic as she counted up the coins.

"Good. That's all right," she said as she dropped the change into her purse.

"You did very well. You can have a bit of pocket money," she said, handing them each a penny.

"I suppose you're hungry now," she added.

"Yes. I'm starving!" answered Ash.

"Have we got any biscuits?" asked Violet.

"You two will eat us out of house and home," a voice said as their older sister came in.

"Oh hello, Claire," said Violet. "Where have you been?"

"In Ludlow. I had some clothes coupons to use so I went in on the bus."

"Did you get anything nice to wear?" asked Violet.

"Believe it or not, I did! I'll show you later," she answered, holding out a large shopping bag. "I simply *must* have a cup of tea first though."

"You know those Gypsies that are camping by the black-smiths," Violet began, as they sat around the old pinewood table drinking tea and eating digestive biscuits. "Well…"

When she had finished telling how they had helped get the sixpence back, her mother seemed surprised.

"That was good of them. I wouldn't have thought they would go out of their way to do a thing like that," she commented.

"No. Me neither," agreed Claire, "I'm sure that must have been old Granny Lovesmith, but I don't know who the girl is."

"Her name's Florence," said Ash.

"Probably a granddaughter," concluded their Mother. "Anyway, I must thank them."

"And you!" she pointed to Violet. "You be more careful in future. We haven't got money to throw away. And that goes for you as well, Ashford. You're the oldest. Don't let it happen again."

"Sorry," they responded in unison.

"Alright, we'll say no more about it. Ash, go and see to the geese and hens. Violet, you can help me in the kitchen."

Ash emptied the scraps of bread and uncooked vegetable peelings from the kitchen into a bucket and went out into the back garden. The garden path led away from the house, with flower borders on either side. At the end of the path, a gate led into the orchard, which gave the Orchard House its name. Old apple trees made up most of the orchard, leaning this way and that, having been battered by the winter winds for many years.

As soon as Ash stepped through the gate, he was greeted by the harsh cries of the three hungry geese who came waddling awkwardly towards him with outstretched wings. He scattered some of the food on the grass and stood watching for a moment as they gobbled it up. They didn't need much extra food at this time of the year with the grass growing fast but their appetites were enormous.

Hens appeared, running from all directions, as he called to them, rattling the bucket as an extra encouragement. They followed him into a wire netting pen and gathered around his feet as he emptied the bucket of scraps into a trough. He counted them, and then checked to see if there were any eggs in the wooden hen house. He found five. Two were still warm, and he was pleased to see they were all fairly clean with only an odd bit of muck and straw sticking to the shells. It wouldn't take him long to wipe them clean. He placed the eggs carefully in the bottom of the bucket then let himself out of the pen and closed the gate securely. Later in the evening, he would come and shut the hens in the henhouse and the geese in the pen, where they would be safe from the fox until they were let out next morning.

The Reverend Clifton Wren, meanwhile, had just returned to the rectory after spending an enjoyable couple of hours in search of the pied flycatcher.

"How did you get on?" his wife enquired as he hung his binoculars on a coat hook in the hallway.

"No luck I'm afraid, but I did see a lesser spotted woodpecker," he replied. "I'll have to remember to make a note of it in my journal. Must spend an hour working on my sermon, before tea though."

Later that evening, as they sat listening to the radio, he remembered the scene outside the garage.

"I forgot to mention a rather unpleasant encounter I witnessed this morning," he began. "I was on my way to look for the pied flycatcher and just as I got to the garage, Robert Westwood was coming out in that new sports car and an elderly woman and a young girl, (Gypsies, I believe,) were standing in his way. They were shouting at one another. It really was most unpleasant. The woman was saying something about how young Westwood had caused them to have an accident yesterday. He was quite abusive and eventually drove away in the most reckless manner."

"Oh dear, what is the world coming to?" his wife replied. "As if there isn't enough trouble in the world as it is. What's wrong with people I wonder? And as for Robert Westwood, he should be ashamed of himself, racing around the town in that car without any thought for other people's safety."

"Yes, he's not been the same since he came back."

"What exactly happened?" Janet asked.

31

"Well, as you know, he was flying bombing raids and one night, his plane got hit and sadly, the navigator was killed. Somehow, Robert managed to nurse the plane back and the rest of the crew were able to parachute safely. By the time they were all out, the plane had lost so much height that when Robert jumped, the parachute didn't have enough time to slow his descent fully and he was lucky to escape with a dislocated shoulder and a couple of cracked ribs."

"Imagine what that sort of experience might do to someone. It's bound to have had an effect on him," the vicar concluded.

"Still, that's no excuse for endangering other people's lives, is it?"

"No, I quite agree. It isn't an excuse, but I think it may be the reason, and psychological problems can take longer to heal than broken bones."

"I hear he's been seeing Claire Sinton lately. I just hope she's not getting carried away. She's only seventeen after all."

"Mmm, I wonder what her mother thinks about it?" the vicar mused.

"I don't imagine she'll be happy about it but perhaps it won't come to anything. You know what young people are like these days. Anyway, I'll find out tomorrow. I'm going to visit."

"Oh good, and I really should have a quiet word with the major."

"Well, why not speak to him tomorrow after the morning service?"

"Yes. I will, Janet. Grasp the nettle, so to speak."

"Good. That's settled then. Time for bed now, I think. Are you coming up?"

"I think I'll just get a breath of air first, now that it's cooled down," he replied.

Clifton Wren stepped out into the vicarage garden and looked up at the moon and stars above. The night sky never failed to fill him with awe as he tried to grasp the enormity of space and time that it revealed. He felt completely insignificant and yet, at the same time, completely at one with creation and with God.

Just as he was about to go back in, he caught sight of a ghostly white form floating over the graveyard next to the garden. As he watched, the barn owl glided silently away across the moonlit meadows towards the old barn.

"Tyto Alba. The barn owl," he said to himself as he quietly closed the back door behind him. "Well, that's made my day."

Chapter 4

Sunday morning dawned with no sign of rain. A few high clouds drifted over the valley through an otherwise empty blue sky.

Ash and Violet had already washed, dressed and eaten breakfast before the church bells rang out across the town. They fed the hens and geese and let them out of the pen into the orchard. They found a few more eggs laid during the night and replaced the dirty nesting straw with fresh. Their chores were done, and they now had some free time before getting ready for church.

Ash had been given a bike for his birthday in April. It was second hand and a bit too big for him, but he could reach the pedals with the seat set as low as it would go, and he loved being out on it whenever he could. That morning, he planned to cycle along the lane to one of his favourite haunts: a wood where he had found a sparrow hawk's nest, last spring.

He was surprised and disappointed to find that he had a flat tyre, and so his morning was spent repairing the puncture instead of enjoying the freedom offered by the quiet back-roads. Violet watched as her brother removed the oily chain and undid the rear wheel nuts. Once the wheel was free, Ash had to lever the tyre off to get to the inner tube. He did this with a couple of spoons from the kitchen that were already bent from previous puncture repairs. Eventually, the inner tube was extracted and Ash traced the leak by submerging it in a bowl of water and watching for the tell-tale stream of bubbles.

By the time the puncture was repaired and the wheel and chain replaced, there was no hope of a bike ride that morning.

"Hurry up you two, or we'll be late for church," their mother called.

Ash groaned, "Why do we have to go every Sunday?" he asked as they went indoors.

"Because I say so," came the answer. "Anyway, it might do you some good if you listened to the vicar's sermon for once instead of fidgeting about as though you'd got ants in your pants. I want you to behave today, understand?"

"Yes, but…"

"No buts! Behave! Now go and get that oil off your hands, and *do not* get the towel filthy."

When Ash had scrubbed as much of the black oil from his hands as he could, he shook the water off and carefully patted them dry, leaving only a faint shadow on the towel. He then changed into his Sunday clothes. He presented himself for inspection and having passed his mother's hasty check, they set out to walk the short distance to St Christopher's together with Violet.

The church was a humble stone structure that boasted no unnecessary decoration. It sat in harmony with the surrounding countryside and might easily go unnoticed to passers-by if it were not for the slightly warped wooden steeple that looked down on the mossy headstones and crosses in the churchyard. Its exact age was unclear, but as it was recorded in the Domesday Book in 1086, it was known to be well over eight-hundred-years old. Some said more like a thousand. Whatever its true age, the church still was not as old as the mighty yew tree that stood next to it. That might even have witnessed Roman soldiers marching past, the school headmaster believed. The ancient place of worship had acquired an atmosphere of peace and tranquillity through the centuries that even the raucous cries of the nesting rooks in the nearby sweet chestnut trees could not disturb.

When they arrived at the church gate, they saw Mrs Evans bustling towards them wearing her Sunday best hat and gloves with a grey skirt and matching jacket. Her stout shoes crunched across the gravel as they walked up the church path together.

"Did you hear about that awful fracas outside the garage yesterday, Beryl?" she asked. "Well, if you ask me," she continued, not waiting for a reply, "it's absolutely typical of that sort of person. No decorum, you see. It never used to be like this. Sytchford always used to be such a quiet place, but now, now, well, where will it end? I was only saying to my husband, the other day, 'Stanley,' I said, '**Stanley**, (he's hard of hearing, you know) where will it end?' I said."

By now, they had reached the church porch.

"I don't know," Beryl Sinton managed to say as Mrs Evans paused for breath. "But from what I heard; Robert Westwood was behaving very badly."

"Robert Westwood? I wasn't referring to Robert Westwood!" Mrs Evans exclaimed as she turned to take her usual place in the church.

"Phew. Some people. No wonder Mr Evans is deaf," whispered Violet as they sat down on a pew on the opposite side of the aisle.

It was surprisingly chilly inside the little church. The sun had not yet evaporated the dew from the grass in the churchyard, and the thick stonewalls of the church would take all morning to warm through.

Ash looked about him and shivered.

The church began to fill, and the murmur of voices grew steadily until the vicar greeted the congregation and invited them to stand and sing the first hymn.

Throughout the service, Ash's thoughts kept returning to the barn and what he and Violet had seen there. What did it mean? He was sure that something was going on in secret. But, what? And what should they do about it?

If they spoke to their mother or any other adult about it, they would immediately want to know why they were in the barn in the first place. They would be in trouble straight away. No, they would have to investigate it themselves, but they needed help. Someone more grown up but not an adult, he concluded.

The lads who had tried to steal the sixpence would know what to do, but the thought of confiding in Nodder and his mates was out of the question. As his mind grappled with this problem, the vicar's voice filtered into his consciousness.

"And so," the vicar was saying, "at this most difficult time of hardship and danger, I know that the people of Sytchford, like good Samaritans, will show generosity and friendship to those worse off than themselves. We will welcome those who are now arriving in our community from wherever they come to work together..."

That's it! That's who we need to speak to! thought Ash.

Violet was not so sure when her brother presented her with his brainwave as they walked home together from church.

"We don't know her, do we? How do we know if we can trust her?" she reasoned. "We need to get to know her better first *if* you're so sure there is something going on. That's what I think anyway."

"How are we goin' to do that?"

Violet thought for a moment. "I know. Mom wants to thank them for what they did. So, why don't we take them some eggs?"

"What are you two whispering about?" their mother asked as she caught up with them at the churchyard gate.

"We were just wondering if we had any eggs to spare, we could take them to the Gypsies as a thank you," answered Violet.

"I think that's an excellent idea. We could spare half a dozen, I'm sure. It's nice to see you thinking of others. Was it the vicar's sermon that gave you the idea?"

"I suppose so," replied Violet uncertainly.

"See I *do* listen sometimes," Ash said proudly.

"You two run on ahead and put the kettle on. I won't be long."

She waited by the church gate as they raced off. Shortly afterwards, she was joined by a large fair-haired man, and together they walked slowly towards orchard house.

"Good morning Mrs Sinton. You wish to speak to me about Ash's progress at school I believe?" began the headmaster.

"Yes, Mr Llewelyn. I'm concerned that he doesn't seem interested in his schoolwork anymore."

"Mm. Well, I wouldn't worry too much. He could do better of course if only he concentrated on one thing for more than ten seconds but he'll grow out of it, I'm sure."

"But what about his reading? Why does he get his words so mixed up? Even simple words. And his spelling is awful!"

"Oh, that's quite usual for lads his age. Nothing to be concerned about, Mrs Sinton. Rest assured, Ash will soon catch up when he puts his mind to it."

Ash's mother was far from certain about that, but Mr Llewelyn knew Ash well, and so she decided not to press the matter further.

The vicar, meanwhile, was chatting to Major Westwood near the church doorway.

"Can we have a word about Robert?" the vicar began. "I hope you don't mind me saying this, but I've been concerned about his behaviour lately. He seems to be…"

"I'm fully aware of my son's behaviour, vicar, but when you think of what he's been through, it's hardly surprising. He's on a short fuse. No one's been hurt. He may have put a few backs up, but some people are a bit too quick to criticise if you ask me," the major fumed.

"I hope you don't think that I'm criticising Robert. It's only the fact that I hold him in such high regard that I felt compelled to discuss this with you," the vicar responded.

The major dropped his guard.

"Mm, well, to tell you the truth, I have been worried about him. Since he came home, he hasn't had one night's sleep that has not been disturbed by nightmares. His nerves are shot to pieces, vicar. He tries to hide it, of course and he wouldn't thank me for confiding in you but I know this won't go any further. He has received a posting to Lincolnshire though, to train new recruits. So, at least he won't be flying any more bombing raids."

"That's good news. It might be just what he needs," replied the vicar. "He's made of stern stuff, Major. I'm sure he'll come through this."

Shortly afterwards, the two men shook hands and went their separate ways, feeling that the air had been cleared.

Chapter 5

That afternoon Violet and Ash set out along the lane to the gypsy site behind the smithy, feeling apprehensive and not at all sure of what sort of welcome they would get. Violet carried six new eggs in a basket.

Their way led past the church and the vicarage that lay behind a high redbrick wall. They could hear the whir of lawnmower blades as the vicar pushed the mower across his beloved croquet lawn in front of the house. A turtle dove purred drowsily from high up in an old pear tree by the side of the lane. Then they heard a low growl, which quickly got louder, and three army trucks roared past, shattering the peaceful atmosphere.

The children stepped back into the vicarage gateway to let them pass and saw armed soldiers sitting in the back of the covered trucks as they disappeared round a bend. Soon, the noise faded away and peace returned. It was almost as if nothing had happened, but Ash and Violet were full of excitement at the intrusion of the war into their quiet lives.

"What on earth was that awful noise?" a voice asked from behind them.

They turned to see the vicar's wife Janet Wren.

"Three army trucks with soldiers. They had rifles and helmets and they went that way," said Ash excitedly, pointing towards the smithy.

"Goodness. We don't see that sort of thing very often. I wonder where they're going."

"I bet they're going to the prisoner of war camp at Penny Heath," said Ash.

"I bet they had a load of prisoners, and that's why there were soldiers with rifles. In case they try to escape."

"Yes, you could well be right," agreed Janet Wren. "And where are you two going?"

"We're going to see a friend," said Violet. "We're taking her some eggs."

"She's a Gypsy," her brother added.

"Oh really? How nice. Is your mother at home this afternoon? I've been meaning to pay her a visit but not got round to it somehow."

"Yes, she said she was going to be working in the garden when we left," replied Violet.

"Oh good. I mustn't keep you from your errand though. Goodbye now."

"Goodbye, Mrs Wren," they answered in unison as they went on their way.

The smithy stood by the roadside just round the next bend. A rough track led down the side to a patch of waste ground where the caravan and tent stood.

When the children got there, they saw Nelson standing in the shade of a tree while the goat was carefully nibbling away at a spiky gorse bush. Two hens were scratching about under the caravan, but there was no sign of Florence or anyone else.

"Now what do we do?" asked Ash.

"HELLO!" shouted Violet. "ANYONE HERE?"

Florence appeared in the doorway of the caravan.

"What do you want?" she called out.

"We just wanted to thank you for what you did yesterday," replied Ash.

"You said thank you yesterday."

"Yes, but we thought you might like a few eggs."

"We've got eggs. We don't need any charity," said Florence abruptly.

"No. We know that. It's not charity. Honestly, it's just to say thank you," Violet responded.

"Did I hear someone say eggs?" asked Gran as she came up behind them. "We could do with a few. Our fowl aren't laying after that fright they had on Friday. Florence, go and put the kettle on and make our guests welcome."

"Violet and Ash, isn't it? Ever been in a vardo before?"

41

"What's a vardo?" asked Violet.

"That's what we call caravans," said Gran. "Do you want to see inside?"

"Oh yes, please!" said Violet.

"Go on in then. Mind the steps."

"Well, what do you think?" she asked when they were all inside.

"It's beautiful!" exclaimed Violet as she looked around.

"You won't see another one like it. We're the last to live like this. All the youngsters are goin' for them tin things. This was handmade. Mind you, it's not as big as some. Could do with a bit more space while Florence is with us, but we squeeze in somehow. Granddad likes to sleep in the bender anyway."

"What's a bender?" Ash asked.

"The tent. He gets hazel rods and bends 'em over, see? Covers 'em with tarpaulin and bob's your uncle. Come and 'ave a look."

Meanwhile, Florence had filled the kettle with fresh water and hung it over the campfire. She poked the embers back to life and threw more wood onto them, and soon the kettle was boiling and a fresh pot of tea was ready.

They all sat in the shade of the caravan as they drank from tin mugs and listened to Gran's stories of life on the road.

Eventually, Gran got to her feet.

"I'm goin' to have a lie down for a bit, so I'll say cheerio. Don't forget to thank your mother for the eggs. It was very thoughtful," she said as she climbed the caravan's steps.

"We won't forget. Thank you for letting us see inside your home," said Violet.

"It was brilliant," added Ash.

When the three children were alone, Violet turned to Florence and said, "She's nice, your gran. Where's your Mom though?"

"She's down south. Kent."

"What about your dad?" asked Ash.

"He's not with us," Florence answered.

"Our dad's not with us either. He's in the air force. He went missing in Italy. We don't know what's happened to him. It's been months since we heard any news," said Ash, sadly.

"That must be 'orrible," Florence said. "At least, I know where my dad is."

"Where is he?" asked Violet.

"In prison," she answered simply.

There was a moment of stunned silence, and then Ash and Violet both spoke at once.

"Why? What did he do?"

"Nothing. 'E bought a ring for my Ma off a bloke 'e knew, that's all. It turned out to be stolen, so 'e got nicked. 'E got three years in prison for it."

"That's not fair," exclaimed Ash indignantly.

"Ma says 'e should 'ave known. Said 'e was too stupid for words. She wouldn't speak to 'im, she was so mad."

"Still, three years in jail for making a mistake. It's not as though he actually stole anything," Ash said.

"Well, we've just got to get on with it. 'E's only got another year to do. It would have been less if 'e'd said who 'e bought it off. But 'e never would."

"How did the police find out?" asked Violet.

"That's a very good question. Someone must have grassed on 'im. If we ever find out who it was, they're goin' to regret it!" Florence said through clenched teeth.

"Did what on him?" asked Violet, genuinely puzzled by the unfamiliar term.

"Told on 'im," Florence explained.

Meanwhile, Janet Wren was in deep conversation with Beryl and Claire Sinton in the kitchen at Orchard House.

"How do you feel about having Italian POWs around?" Janet asked. "There's a rumour going about that they're going to start sending them out to help with farm work."

"I don't mind so long as they keep themselves to themselves, but I don't like the idea. I know it might not be very Christian of me, but I can't help the way I feel."

"I understand, Beryl. I'd feel just the same if I was in your place. It must be so *difficult* for you all."

"It's not knowing anything. That's the hardest part of it all. I feel that he *is* alive, but it's been months now. Why haven't we heard anything?"

"You mustn't give up hope. I'm *sure* he *will* be alright," Janet said as positively as she could.

"Oh. I won't. That's all we can do, isn't it, Claire?"

"Yes. Hope and pray," replied her daughter as the two sat holding hands across the table.

Violet and Ash walked home later that afternoon, in awe of their new friend.

Someone had entered their lives from another world.

She knew about things that they had only ever read in the newspapers before, and she had experienced so much more than they, or any of their friends, had.

It was hard to believe that she was just the same age as Ash.

He felt that their discovery of the tinned food in the old barn was somehow trivial by comparison with what Florence had just told them.

"But it is important!" insisted Violet. "Somebody's holding out on the rest of us and I want to know who it is. Whose barn is it?"

"Joseph Leonard owns it. You know, he's got Phoenix Farm. You don't think it's him, do you?"

"I don't know, but I'm going to find out. You know I'm meeting Florence tomorrow after school. Well, what if I ask her to come with us to take another look in the old barn? We might find a clue."

"I thought you didn't want to go back there."

"I don't, but when I think that someone in the village is keeping all that food to themselves, it makes me so cross! It's like… like, they're not on our side! They're just another enemy."

Chapter 6

Violet and Florence went shopping together as arranged and managed to get nearly everything they were sent for, except sugar, which Mrs Evans promised would be in "any day soon". When they got back to Orchard House, Violet said she had something to show Florence.

"Come and see what we've got," she said, excitedly.

She led her friend through the garden into the orchard and opened the hen house door.

Florence saw in the dim light a brown hen sitting in a nest box. There were high-pitched cheeping noises coming from underneath the mother hen who was doing her best to protect her chicks from the intruders. She fluffed out her feathers and spread her wings, but there were too many chicks to control, and tiny yellow balls of fluff kept popping out from under her, staggering about on spindly legs.

The girls knelt down for a closer look.

"'Ow many do you think there are?" asked Florence.

"Well, there were twelve eggs, but they might not all hatch. We'll soon know when they start running about on their own. They're beautiful, aren't they?"

"I think they're the best things I've ever seen!" agreed Florence. "Thank you for showing 'em to me."

"I *knew* you'd like them," said Violet.

"It's a shame about the sugar still not being in," Violet said as she shut the hen house door.

"It seems that most things are getting harder to find. I'd love a tin of baked beans. You wouldn't think that is *too* much to ask, would you?" replied Florence.

"What would you say if I told you that someone in the village has got a load of tinned food hidden away?"

"I wouldn't be surprised. Everybody's on the fiddle these days if you ask me. It's the only way to get by," Florence replied knowingly.

"This is more than that. It's selfish and mean! There's a traitor in Sytchford and I'm going to find out who it is!" Violet exclaimed.

"Who do you think it is anyway?"

"I don't know yet, but I'm investigating. Do you want to help?"

"I might. Were there any baked beans?"

"Baked beans, sausages, corned beef, peaches…"

"I ain't never 'ad any peaches. What are they like?"

"I can't describe them, but they're just the most *delicious* things in the whole world, *and* they're in this lovely syrup," Violet replied.

"Alright. What do you want me to do?"

Violet and Ash met Florence at the smithy that Friday evening, and they made their way along the lane to the old barn. When they got there, they found the gate to the field open and the sheep gone. The barn doors were unlocked, so Ash and Florence went cautiously in while Violet kept watch.

There was no sign of the boxes of tinned food. Instead, they found a plough and other farm implements that he was sure had not been there before.

"They were just over there. Stacked in the corner," said Ash, pointing to the place where he had found them. "Honestly."

"Let's 'ave a good look round. They might 'ave been moved somewhere else," suggested Florence.

They searched the barn from end to end, but the hoard of tinned food had gone.

"So what do we do now?" Ash asked, as they walked back towards the smithy.

"Well, we know who owns the barn, don't we?" said Violet.

"Who?" asked Florence.

"Mr Leonard," said Ash.

"Joseph Leonard? The farmer?"

"Yes. Do you know him?"

"Granddad's goin' to be workin' for 'im next week. I might be goin' over there meself."

"See what you can find out then when you're there," suggested Violet.

"Alright, I'll keep me eyes open. See what I can see. I wouldn't mind finding a few tins of baked beans… or peaches," she added wistfully.

Early Monday morning, Florence and Granddad set out together, on foot, towards the village. When they came to the crossroads, they turned right along a quiet narrow road towards Phoenix Farm. In places, the lane was overhung with gnarled old damson trees bearing tiny green fruit.

They walked between ancient hedgerows made up mainly of hawthorn, hazel, elm, sycamore and holly.

"You can tell 'ow old an edge is by the number of different sorts of trees in 'im," Granddad observed. "I reckon this one must be five 'undred years old at least."

He pointed out the different species as they continued on their way, adding what uses they could be put to. Each one had its own value apart from helping to make a sturdy hedge. Some provided food in the form of fruit or nuts. Many could be used for medicines, whether from the leaves, fruit, bark or even roots. Each type of tree provided wood with a variety of uses, from manufacturing gunpowder to making chair legs to building ships and every other thing imaginable. The hedgerows and woods were Florence's schoolroom and her grandparents had become her teachers.

Her formal education had been patchy as she had never lived in one town for long enough to get settled into school. Time after time, she would just be getting used to one, and then they would be off to another town or village, and the process would begin all over again. Florence dreaded the thought of school now. She had been treated with contempt by too many children, as well as their parents, to make her never want to go back to one. Her grandparents knew enough about what it was like for her, and they hoped she would go unnoticed by the authorities. If and when the authorities did take an interest and insisted, she attend, then she would have to. But for the time being, they were quite happy to let things stay as they were.

They came to a place where the hedges were all but hidden by tall feathery cow parsley with its creamy white flower heads filling the early morning air with a sharp sweet scent.

"Don't be mistakin' cow parsley for wild parsnip nor hemlock. Hemlock be deadly poison," Granddad warned.

"I'm not daft, Granddad," she replied. "Diff'rent thing altogether. Hemlock grows in boggy places. It's bigger. It smells different. It…"

"All right. All right. I can see you're not goin' to poison yourself," Granddad laughed.

The road dropped down to where a shallow stream flowed across, then rose steeply again on the other side. The stream murmured softly as it slid beneath a large flat slab of stone that served as a footbridge. On either side of the road, tall beach trees spread their leafy branches over the ford creating a cool, shaded spot where bluebells and wild garlic flourished in profusion. There was only the musical sound of the stream to disturb the silence, and Florence felt as though she had walked into a church. There was something else: a sense that they were not entirely alone. It was as though their arrival had interrupted something. For some reason, she imagined herself an uninvited guest at some unseen event.

They paused on the stone bridge and looked around. "This be a fairy-dell, Granddad," she whispered.

"Tis so. That were what your Gran said very first time she saw it," he replied.

They stood still for a while listening to the stream beneath their feet until the sound of a cuckoo calling somewhere close by broke the spell and they continued on their way, climbing the steep winding road in silence until they finally emerged from the leafy hollow into the fresh open air. Here, a side road, little wider than a hay wagon, branched off to the left.

"'Ere we are. Farm's just round the bend," Granddad said as they turned into the lane.

They passed by a meadow where a herd of cattle munched on the lush grass and buttercups. They were unlike any cattle Florence had seen before.

"Longhorns," Granddad informed her. "Beautiful, ain't they?"

Florence agreed, impressed by the size of their long curving horns and the variety of shades in their brindled hides.

The black and white, half-timbered farmhouse stood facing them as they walked through the gateway between barns and outbuildings that flanked the farmyard. A pair of white fantail doves took off from where they were feeding amongst a few clucking hens and circled overhead before landing on the thatched farmhouse roof. A cockerel crowed loudly as it stood fearlessly regarding Florence and Granddad with black, beady eyes as though they were trespassing on its territory, which of course they were.

Two great chestnut coloured heads appeared above a stable door as the draft horses came to see who was disturbing the peace.

"Suffolk Punches. Finest 'orses anywhere in the world for pullin' the plough I reckon. And these are two of the best you'll ever see: Samson and Goliath," Granddad said as he went over and stroked the nose of the nearest horse.

"Morning, Herby," said a cheerful voice, as a grey-haired man appeared from a nearby doorway. He was tall-ish, slightly built, with thick eyebrows and a well-trimmed moustache below a slightly curved nose, which, Florence thought, gave him a hawkish look. He had bright blue eyes set in a sun-tanned face with crow's feet that spoke of a life outdoors and a sense of humour.

"Ah. Mornin', Joe. A fine mornin' it is too. This 'ere's our granddaughter Florence, as I was tellin' you about," Granddad replied turning towards her.

"Florence, this is Mr Leonard. E's got work for us."

"I have. But first let's go inside and have a cup of tea and a chat about things. I've been up for a couple of hours and could do with a brew."

Inside the farmhouse, the kettle was soon whistling on the range as Joe's wife, Bryony, laid out the mugs, sugar and milk. The plump, cheerful woman immediately made them feel at ease before she left to see to the chickens and collect the eggs.

Granddad and Joe talked of this and that, mainly horses. Granddad had been a horse trader all his life and Joe Leonard had been breeding Suffolk Punches for most of his, so they had a lot in common.

Florence looked around the comfortable kitchen and wondered if it was likely that Joseph Leonard would have anything to do with the hoard of tinned food. She quickly decided that he would not. For one thing, he would have no need and, in any case, he didn't give her the impression that he had anything to hide. If he had, why invite her and Granddad into the house? After all, most people wouldn't invite Gypsies in under any circumstances.

The kitchen was bathed in sunlight that streamed through the open door and windows. The walls and ceiling were whitewashed. Red tiles covered the floor. There was no carpet, and the scrubbed pine table and a few odd chairs were the only furniture. Overhead, heavy oak beams divided the whitewashed ceiling into three, and from one of the beams a ham hung from a hook. One wall was lined with shelves on which stood jars of pickles and preserves, and pots and pans of all shapes and sizes.

Through an open door, Florence could see into the living room where a grandfather clock and other pieces of dark polished furniture glowed where the light caught them.

She saw an armchair and a settee covered in a floral-patterned material, and it occurred to her that she had never in all her life been in such a well-off home.

"Well, I've got plenty of work that needs to be done. Everyone's shorthanded at the moment," she heard the farmer say. "But wouldn't she be better off going to school? I'll have a word with the headmaster if you like."

To her relief, Granddad shook his head.

"Oh, I don't think she'd like that," he muttered.

"What do you say, Florence? Shall I see if I can get you a place at the village school?"

"No! Please, mister. Don't make me go to school!" she replied without a moment's thought.

Joseph was startled by the vehemence with which the girl spoke. He could see that she was fearful of schools and guessed she probably had some good reason.

"Let's forget about school for now. You can start work for me but only for three days a week. How does that suit you?"

Florence looked at Granddad. He nodded.

The first task assigned to Florence was to join the other workers hoeing in the hop fields.

Hoeing was hard, monotonous work that caused her hands to blister. At first, she went home tired and miserable at the end of each day, but she was not going to give up. There were other women and girls working in the fields with Florence, though none as young as she was. Some came from the village but one or two were land army girls who were volunteering to help with the war effort. For the first time in her life, Florence was meeting people from outside of her own Gypsy life, and she was beginning to enjoy their company. They were all equal in the fields, wherever they came from.

Her gran made up an ointment from self-heal, comfrey and other wild plants she had collected and treated her blisters with it. They soon began to heal and her hands grew hard. She was determined to keep up with the older girls, and when pay-day came, she felt proud to take home the small amount that she had worked so hard for.

Chapter 7

A few days after Florence and Granddad's visit, another new-comer appeared at Phoenix Farm. This one arrived unexpectedly on the back of an army truck.

The handsome, dark-eyed young man jumped down and landed lightly on his feet and then reached up and took down a kit bag. He wore a grey shirt with the sleeves rolled up, exposing sun-tanned forearms. His trousers and cap were of some rough grey cloth and the jacket was slung over one shoulder. Circular red patches were sewn onto his shirt and jacket so that there could be no mistaking that he was a prisoner of war.

"This is where you're billeted from now on! You stay put! Understand?" the truck driver shouted from the cab.

"Si. I work 'ere. I live 'ere," responded the prisoner.

The truck drove away in a cloud of dust.

He looked around and saw a man coming across the yard, leading two great draft horses.

The man stopped in front of him and smiled, and the horses halted and stood patiently without need of any word of command.

"Who are you?" enquired the man in a surprised tone.

"Salvatore Bonelli. Call me Salvo. I am sent 'ere. To work. They tell me I stay 'ere. We all leave the camp. Go different places. I work for you. Yes?"

"Ah. I see. You're from the POW camp at Penny Heath."

"Si. Penny 'eath."

"That's typical. I've been trying to get some help from Penny Heath for months, without any luck. Now you turn up out of the blue expecting to be put up here."

"No one tell you?"

"No one tells us anything these days. Never mind, we'll sort it out."

"My name's Joseph Leonard," the farmer continued, holding out his hand. "I'm glad you're here, even if we weren't expecting you. Ever done any farm work before, Salvo?"

"Since I am in England, I work on the land but not with the cows."

"I dare say you'll get the hang of it soon enough. You'll be working with Herby. He'll show you the ropes. Won't you, Herby?" Joseph said as Granddad came up to them wheeling a barrow piled high with manure. "Do as he says and we'll all get along fine."

"I'm goin' to start ploughing Lower meadow Herby."

"That's a sad thing to 'ave to do," Granddad observed.

"Can't be helped, Herby. Ministry orders. We've got to grow more spuds and that's that. I've no say in the matter. It should have been done by now, but there's still just enough time if I can get the ground prepared this week. Then you two can help get 'em planted."

They watched as Joseph Leonard led the horses away.

Salvatore turned to Granddad, "OK. Where are ropes?"

Granddad smiled, "Not real ropes. It's just a sayin'. It means I teach you what to do. How did you end up here in Sytchford anyway?"

"I live in small town in mountains. Very beautiful. I work in garage. I fix the cars. I am... what is the word?"

"A mechanic?" offered Granddad.

"Si, a mechanic. So, one day I get call up papers, and I 'ave to leave. They send me off to Libya to fix tanks in desert."

"Where's Libya?"

"North of Africa. Very 'ot. Inside tanks like oven. We go to Egypt. No problem. See pyramids. Soon British attack and we try to go back. Get cut off. So I am captured in big battle. I am lucky though. Many friends killed."

"How long ago was that then?" asked Granddad.

"Two years. Since then I am prisoner."

"What about your family? Do they know where you are?"

53

"I 'ave written, but I do not know if they get letters. I 'ave not 'ad a reply," Salvo said sadly.

"Ever think about escape?"

"At first, every day, but now I decide to stay till war finish. 'Ees not so bad, and what would 'appen if I try? Capture again, and then they put me in place not so good. No. One day I go back 'ome. When war finish."

"Well I 'ope that day comes soon! It's gone on too long. I remember the Great War. That was supposed to put an end to wars they said, but 'ere we are again. Joe Leonard. He was in that one an all. One of the lucky ones. Got through it, somehow and came 'ome but lots didn't."

"War is a terrible thing. When-a-we gonna learn that?" the Italian responded.

"Don't ask me. I dunno if we ever will."

"You not same as people 'ere I think. Where you from, 'Erby?"

"That's a good question. Everywhere and nowhere. I'm a Gypsy. A Romany. A traveller, see?"

"Ah. I understand. Not good to be Romany now in my country. You lucky to be 'ere. I think maybe we both lucky. So! What we do first, 'Erby?"

"Well, we start by muckin' out the cowshed. You might not think you'm so lucky by the time we finish that, I can tell you!"

Lower meadow had never been ploughed before as far as anyone could recall, but then there had never been such a serious shortage of food before either, and so, together with countless other meadows across the country, lower meadow was turned over to the production of crops.

Joseph Leonard was not happy about having to do it, but it wasn't a matter of choice. Nevertheless, he regretted having to tell his tenant to remove the sheep at such short notice, and the barn owl would probably have to find a new home for the time being as well. So it was with a heavy heart, that he harnessed the two heavy horses to the plough and set to work turning the green grass under the soil. It took four days to plough the whole meadow. He could have done it in half the time with a tractor, but it would not start, no matter who tried, and so it was sitting idle in the farmyard while the horses plodded tirelessly up and down the meadow with Joe guiding the plough. He didn't mind having to use the horses. In fact, he preferred working that way even if it did take longer.

He worked the field in such a way that when finished, the plough had formed the ridges necessary for the potatoes to be planted deep within. The Suffolk Punches were turned out to pasture for a well-earned rest and the next day, the planting began.

Meanwhile, Granddad and Salvo were getting along famously.

In September 1943, Italy had surrendered to the allies and then declared war on Germany, so Granddad was happy to treat the Italian POWs as friends. After all, he reasoned, they were now on the same side, and anyway, what did it matter? Italians or Germans, when it came down to it, Herby found they were generally no different to anyone else. Just caught up in something they had no say in.

The authorities had other ideas though, and while they allowed the POWs more freedom and paid them for their work, they were still prisoners, and their movements were restricted. Most importantly, relationships with young women were strictly forbidden.

Fortunately, Joseph Leonard had converted one of the stables into a dormitory for the influx of workers who always arrived at the end of summer for the hop-picking season. It was empty now so Salvo had his pick of the bunk beds and with Bryony Leonard preparing his meals, he felt as though his luck was in. He missed the camaraderie of his fellow POWs though, and hence, he was determined to find a way to meet up with some of them from time to time. One day, he found an old bike lying in one of the farm outbuildings and when he asked, Joe said of course he could use it if he could fix the flat tyres, broken chain and twisted forks. With Herby's help, it took Salvo a week to complete the repairs in his spare time.

His first outing was to the Gypsy campsite, and from then on, he found a new sense of freedom and new friends as well.

Alf Carter and Granddad took him to Cooper's Mill one Sunday morning to fish for carp in the deep pool. Afterwards, they took him to the Crystal Ball and introduced him to some of the locals and to the beer that was brewed in the brew-house behind the pub. The sound of laughter and singing could be heard coming from the pub as the sun shone down on the deserted high street.

Not everyone was on such good terms with the Italian though. He was not welcome everywhere. Beryl Sinton, still waiting for news of her husband, had no desire to befriend someone she still regarded as an enemy, and both Ash and Violet viewed him with suspicion.

Florence was now one of the gang carrying out the back-breaking work of potato planting in Lower Meadow. Florence didn't mind too much. It was a change from hoeing and she was still working alongside the land army girls who were always ready for a laugh and a joke.

On the days she wasn't working in the fields, Florence helped her gran around the campsite. What with cleaning, cooking, shopping and other chores, she had very little time to spare and so, saw nothing of Ash and Violet for a while.

They, of course, had other friends in and around the village, and two of these were often seen in the company of Ash.

Identical twins Frank and Freddy Turner had been his friends since they started school together. The brown-haired, dark-eyed boys were a good head taller than Ash. They had been used to much hard physical work during their short lives and that had toughened them up, and helped make them seem older than their years. Either one, on their own, would have been a match for the likes of Nodder Crump but together, they were a force to be reckoned with. They could easily have ruled the school playground if they had a mind to, but having inherited their mother's friendly good nature, they had no desire to throw their weight around, and it was only in self-defence that they would resort to violence. Ash could remember only one such occasion when Jack Spragg had rashly picked a fight with Freddy. That ended quickly when one well-aimed blow gave his attacker a bloody nose. From then on, the twins were treated with respect by all their schoolmates.

The twins lived with their mother and father in a tiny old cottage down a small lane leading off the road to Phoenix Farm. The cottage at that time had no electricity and was lit by oil lamps. Water came from a pump near the back door. It was a hard life for the inhabitants, especially during the winters.

Their father, Sam, suffered from a long-standing back complaint which defied diagnosis, let alone treatment, and this meant he was rarely able to work more than a day or two at a time.

Their mother, Gertie, had to go out to work in the fields in all weathers to feed and clothe her family. She did this without complaint and, moreover, with good humour.

To make ends meet, Frank and Freddy kept a couple of ferrets and during the winter months, Ash had sometimes joined the twins when they went ferreting.

On frosty mornings, they would arrive at one of the many warrens they knew of in the hedgerows around village. Nets were spread over all the rabbit holes they could find, and then in would go the ferret. Within seconds, the terrified rabbits would bolt for the nearest exit only to be caught in the nets.

One sharp blow to the back of the head was usually enough to despatch the unfortunate creatures, and then came the vile business of gutting the bodies.

Cruel though it may have been, it was only the abundance of rabbits that kept hunger at bay in the Turners' cottage during the long winter months.

Now that spring had arrived, however, the ferrets were not needed, and although the twins were often called upon to help out on the family allotment, the longer hours of daylight meant that they and Ash had time to roam the countryside.

And so it was that Ash hardly noticed Florence's absence, but Violet had grown fond of their new friend and missed her company.

It was her older sister, however, who would soon strike up a friendship with the young Gypsy girl.

Chapter 8

Claire and Robert had not made up after their row, and now that he had been posted far away, she had come to accept that the romance was over.

Still, it was fun while it lasted, she reflected with a smile.

She had begun to feel as though she should be doing something more with her life. What she really wanted was to become an actress. She caught the bus to the nearby town of Ludlow as often as possible to see the latest films and the glamorous film stars who starred in them. She would have joined the amateur dramatics group in Worcester if it wasn't so far, but right now, she knew that it was just not possible and that would have to wait. After the war, things would be different, she told herself. Then she would be free to pursue her dream.

For now, she had a part-time job waiting on in the local tea rooms and had undertaken a correspondence typing course. Otherwise, she did all she could to support her mother at home, but she wanted something more.

Then one day, she was waiting at the bus stop when she overheard a conversation between two land army girls.

"So, when are you leaving, Becky?" one of the girls asked.

"Saturday. It's awful short notice, but Mr Leonard's been ever so good about it. And it can't be helped. These opportunities don't come along every day."

"No. You're jolly lucky. I wish someone would offer me a job in London. But all the same, we're going to miss you."

"I feel bad about going, what with everything that needs doing on the farm, but I can't deny that I won't be glad to see the back of spud planting."

"It is murder, isn't it?" her friend said. "I'll be glad when it's finished."

"I'm sorry to have to leave you to it, Helen, but I'm sure you'll get someone else to take my place. I'll write to let you know how things are going, and I'd love you to visit as soon as I'm settled."

Claire had never really considered farm work before, but the more she thought about it the more the idea appealed to her. It would mean a bit of extra money coming in and a worthwhile contribution to the war effort as well. She talked to her mother about it and she agreed that it would be a good thing for her, at least for the summer months.

So, the very next day, she walked into the farmyard to offer her services to Joseph Leonard.

"I didn't think land work was your sort of thing," the farmer said when she had explained why she had come. "Are you sure you want to take it on? It's hard work. Early starts, and out in all weathers too."

"Yes, I'm sure. I want to do something useful for once. I think it's my duty to do my bit, and to be honest, we could do with the extra money," she answered.

"What does your mother say?"

"I've talked it over with her and she thinks it's a good idea. I won't let you down, I promise."

It was difficult to say no to Claire when she had set her heart on a thing, and despite his reservations, Joseph agreed to take her on, starting next Monday morning.

"Thank you, Mr Leonard. I'll be here at half-past-six. On the dot," she said, turning to leave.

At that moment, there was a loud bang, like a gunshot, from the far corner of the farmyard and the tractor burst into life. A thick plume of oily smoke rose into the air for a moment then cleared as the engine settled down.

"You've done it, Salvo. Well done!" shouted Joseph above the noise.

"Si. She tickin' over nice. I think she fixed," Salvo replied as he slammed the bonnet down and turned towards them with a triumphant smile.

Joseph beckoned him over.

"This is Salvatore. He's been assigned to work here, and I have to say he's proving to be very useful."

"And this is Claire Sinton. She's going to be working here from now on."

"Very pleased to meet you, Miss Sinton," Salvo said politely.

She could only respond with a weak smile.

This was the first time she had come face to face with any Italian. She had imagined that she would feel anger, or even hatred, when she did so, but her first feeling was one of pleasant surprise. This was quickly followed by a sense of disloyalty as she remembered her father.

"Now that the tractor's running, Salvo can pick you up Monday. No need to come up to the farm. We'll be working in the six-acre field, tying in the hops. Orchard House is on the way. That is, if you don't mind sitting on the trailer," said Joseph.

"No. Of course not. I'll wait outside at half-six then, shall I?"

"Bring some sandwiches with you and something to drink. It will be a long day," advised Joseph as they parted company.

Ash could hardly believe his ears when he found out his big sister was going to be working on the farm.

"She won't last five minutes," he said. "She hates getting her hands dirty. It won't work."

"Well, that's where you're wrong!" Violet stated with surprising certainty. "Once she makes her mind up to do something, she does it. Anyway, I'm glad she's doing something to help the war effort and you should be too. I wish I could do something really useful like that."

"You *are* doing something useful already," their mother said. "Both of you. I don't know how I'd manage without your help, and now that Claire's going to be working in the fields, there will be even more for you to do here. Don't worry about that."

Something was still bothering Violet though.

She could not forget the hoard of tinned food they had found in the barn. She thought that if she could somehow find who was behind it, she would have done something useful for the whole village, not just her own family. But she was at a loss as to what to do next. The only suspect was Joseph Leonard because he owned the barn, but she hadn't been able to speak to Florence since she had been going to Phoenix Farm and in any case, she knew deep down that Joseph Leonard would not be mixed up in anything so sneaky. So, how *was* she going to make any progress? She wished her father was with them. He would know what to do.

That evening, Violet sat down on her own at the kitchen table while the others were listening to the radio in the living room. She had with her the photograph album containing the pictures her father had taken while on leave two years previously. She opened the album and studied each photo in turn. The black and white images were mostly of the family. Her father only appeared on two. He had used a tripod and delayed exposure to get himself on the photos, she recalled. As she looked through the pictures, she was surprised at how much younger they all looked, although it seemed like only yesterday that they were taken.

At the back of the album, she came across an envelope containing pictures, which she hadn't looked at before. She glanced at them casually. They were of the village, the church, the school, the abandoned mill and lastly, the old barn.

She was about to put them away when something about the last photograph made her look again. Now it had her full attention, because a car was parked in the doorway of the barn, facing the camera, and she was almost certain she knew who the battered old Austin seven belonged to. She quickly rummaged through the drawers of the sideboard until she found what she needed, then returned to the table and examined the image through the magnifying glass.

She could just read the number plate. She was right. The car belonged to Albert Skinner.

Violet sat back feeling like a proper detective. She had found a clue, but was it *really* a clue? After all, she reasoned, the photo was two years old, and just because Albert Skinner's car was outside the barn, didn't mean he was the hoarder. On the other hand, it was her only lead and she had a duty to follow it up. She called Ash into the kitchen.

"Look. It is Albert Skinner's car, isn't it?" said Violet as Ash examined the photograph that she had laid in front of him.

"Yes. It's his car, alright, but it doesn't prove anything, does it?" he replied.

"I know it doesn't *prove* anything, but it's evidence, and it's worth investigating. I think we should see what we can find out."

"How?"

"Well, we can investigate. Wait till he's gone out and see what we can find at Ivy Cottage. I bet he's hidden it all there."

"I don't know. What if someone sees us?" said her brother who had begun to lose interest in the whole thing as the days went by.

"We won't get caught. One of us can keep watch. It will only take a minute," insisted Violet.

Ash was still reluctant. He knew the sound of every one of the vehicles in the village and the one he heard drive away from the old barn had not sounded like Albert Skinner's Austin Seven. He was about to say so when Violet played her trump card.

"You're not *scared,* are you, Ash? I'll do it on my own if you're too frightened."

"I'm not scared! Course I'm not!" he responded vigorously. "We can do it tomorrow if you like."

"Thanks, Ash. I knew you wouldn't let me down. We'll say we're going to the allotments, and that won't be a lie because we can carry on to the allotments afterwards," she said brightly.

Chapter 9

Officially, Monday was a bank holiday, but that made no difference on the farm where animals needed to be fed and cared for. The hop vines were shooting up as well, and they needed to be tied in to the supports or they would end up on the ground instead of climbing up the wires.

Salvo loaded the trailer with balls of twine, coils of wire, wooden posts and an assortment of tools that would be needed for the day's work, then coupled it to the tractor and drove off to pick up Claire.

She was waiting outside Orchard House, as arranged. She was wearing an old skirt and blouse, boots and a wide-brimmed straw hat to keep the sun off her fair skin. She also had a shoulder bag containing a flask of tea and sandwiches for lunch. She felt decidedly shabby as she waited for Salvo, but there was no point in ruining good clothes in the fields.

She heard the tractor coming along the lane and wondered if she was doing the right thing, but it was too late to turn back now. The little grey tractor and battered trailer came rattling round the corner and stopped with a squeal of brakes. Salvo waved a hand towards the trailer.

"You want me give you 'and up?" he shouted over the noise of the engine.

"No, thanks. I can manage," she replied as she grabbed hold of the side of the trailer and placed one foot on the muddy trailer wheel. She hauled herself up and over into the trailer and sat down on the rusty wheel arch, feeling rather pleased with herself.

The journey to Six Acre field was the most painful she had ever endured. She hung on tightly as the trailer bounced along the bumpy road. "Next time, I'm going to walk," she said to herself. Fortunately, the field was only a short distance away and when they arrived, she saw someone waiting in the gateway.

Salvo stopped and adjusted a lever on the steering column. The engine died down, and he climbed down from his seat and offered her his hand.

"No need, thank you," she said coldly as she climbed gingerly to the ground.

"Miss Florence, Miss Claire," he said to each in turn. "Florence, will show you what to do. I go now. I will come 'ere at-a five o'clock. Take you back. Yes?"

She was about to say that she would rather walk when he added, "I find a somethin' for you to sit on."

"Oh, that would be good. All right. See you then," she heard herself say.

"You're Violet and Ash's sister, ain't you?" asked Florence as they made their way to the rows of hops.

"That's right. And you're the girl who helped them out when they bumped into those louts in the village a few weeks ago, aren't you?"

"Yeah. Can't stand those sort of kids. They think they're so big, but anybody stands up to 'em and they don't know what to do. Got no bottle when it comes to it."

"No, I don't suppose they have," agreed Claire uncertainly, wondering what bottles they were lacking.

"The shoots need to be wound round this way," said Florence as they started work.

"Clockwise. I see. What happens if they're wound anticlockwise?"

"You mean the other way?" asked Florence. "They fall off again."

"So, we've got to do every one? The whole field?"

"That's it. Every one's got to be done."

Claire's heart sank.

"It's easy," said Florence. "Dead borin' but better than plantin' spuds any day. We won't have to do it all by ourselves. There's a land army girl, Helen, and Ma Turner, from the village, she's comin' later on as well."

So, they began the monotonous task of tying in six acres of hop shoots. Helen and Gertie Turner soon joined them, and as they worked their way along the rows, they talked.

They talked about anything and everything to break the monotony of twiddling one shoot after another round their wire supports. To her surprise, Claire realised that Florence was an intelligent girl, and not only that, but good company as well.

"So, what's that Italian POW like?" she finally asked.

"Salvo? 'E's all right. Gets on well with Granddad and Alf. Why?"

"Well, I've never met an Italian before, and we have been fighting a war against them. I don't know if they can be trusted."

"Granddad says they're on our side now, so he oughtn't to be a prisoner of war anyway."

"It's not that simple," said Claire. "My father could be a prisoner of war, or he might even be dead. Killed by the Italians."

"Salvo wouldn't kill a sparrow!" Florence responded hotly.

After a while, the sky clouded over and soon, rain began to fall.

"We might as well have our lunch now while it's rainin'," said Gertie.

They all hurried to the shelter of a corrugated iron hut and watched the rain falling steadily as they ate their sandwiches and drank their lukewarm tea.

"This'll do some good," observed Gertie. "My allotment was beginning to look parched."

"I hope it cools things down a bit. I'm starting to wilt myself," said Claire.

"Don't reckon it's goin' to last long," Florence commented as she scanned the clouds coming in from the west.

"What happens if it *doesn't* stop?" asked Claire.

"We get wet. That's why I always wear me mac and wellie-boots. Never know when it might rain in this country," replied Gertie, sagely.

Claire nodded. Come to think of it, she had never seen Gertie Turner in anything other than the old brown raincoat tied at the waist with a string and Wellingtons with the tops turned down. As she looked out at the rain, it seemed now to make a good deal of sense.

Florence was right. The rain soon blew over and the workers were able to carry on with their task under the hot sun.

Helen had been a typist in Luton before the war, but a year ago, she had been conscripted into the Women's Land Army, and now was adamant that she would never go back to office work.

"I know the war's terrible, but honestly, I've had more fun and met more people. All sorts of people than ever I would have done. Know what I mean?"

"I never looked at it like that," replied Claire. "They do say it's an ill wind that blows no one any good, I suppose."

"Do they?" replied Helen. "All I know is I've made lots of friends with people I would never even have met. Like Rebecca for one. We were billeted together. She's gone back to London now though."

"I know. I'm afraid I overheard you talking about it at the bus stop. I couldn't help hearing what you were saying. I don't usually listen to other peoples conversations," she added hastily. "Anyway, that's what gave me the idea to volunteer and help out in the fields."

"Well, good for you! We need all the help we can get. What were you doing before?"

Soon, they were getting to know each other and a friendship began to grow.

Eventually, as the shadows began to lengthen, they heard the sound of the tractor approaching. It stopped on the road just outside the gate as the workers collected up their things and trudged to meet it.

"You not finish yet?" Salvo asked as he jumped to the ground.

"Only jokin'," he said, holding his hands up in surrender as he observed the weary faces in front of him. "Come on. I take-a-you 'ome."

Chapter 10

Beryl Sinton was getting the washing in off the line when Claire walked slowly down the path after finishing her first day's work in the hop fields.

"You look done in," her mother said seeing her daughter slump onto the bench by the back door.

"That is the most soul-destroying job anyone could ever have to do. And look at my hands," Claire said holding them out in front of her. "How am I ever going to get that horrible stain off?"

Her fingers were indeed very badly stained from the sap of the hop plants, even under the nails which Claire was, as a rule, extremely particular about.

"They smell awful as well," she continued as she sniffed daintily at the offensive odour.

"Oh, I rather like the smell of hops," Beryl replied. "Why don't you go and wash your hands while I make us a nice cup of tea."

Just then Violet came running round the corner of the house.

"Gosh. You've caught the sun," she began. "What did you have to do? Why are your fingers yellow? What's that smell?"

"Leave your sister alone, and let her get cleaned up, then she can tell you all about it later," her mother said. "Where's Ash?"

"He's down by the brook playing on the rope swing with Frank and Freddy," she answered.

"Well, go and call him for tea. It'll be ready soon."

"What are we having?" Violet asked.

"We are having the first of our new potatoes with broad beans and as a special treat you can have two rashers of bacon"

"Each?" Violet asked.

"Each," her mother replied

"Oh great! That's my *absolute* favourite meal in the whole world! Wait till Ash finds out." And with that, she hurried off through the orchard in search of her brother.

Claire sat at the kitchen table enjoying her cup of tea while her mother busied herself at the sink preparing the potatoes and beans.

"I honestly didn't expect it to be that hard," she began once the tea had revived her a little.

"If it really is that bad, perhaps you should think about only doing the rest of the week. I'm sure Joe will soon find someone else to take your place."

"No. I'll get used to it. I can't let him down like that. If Gertie Turner can do it, so can I."

"Was it just the two of you today?"

"No. There was a land army girl called Helen. She's ever so nice. And that Gypsy girl Florence. She puts me to shame when it comes to work."

"What about the Italian POW?"

"Oh, he had to go and do something somewhere else, so we didn't see him again till he picked us up to take us home."

"It isn't that far to walk. You don't really need a lift surely."

"Well, I was really glad of it, coming home. Anyway, it's already arranged for tomorrow, and after that, we might be working somewhere else, so I mightn't get a lift then."

"That Florence is a bright girl," Claire continued, quickly changing the subject.

"She can barely read or write, but she knows all the star signs and their dates and the characteristics that go with them. She says I'm a typical Taurean."

"Well, you can be stubborn enough at times, so I wouldn't argue with her there."

"The thing is it's such a shame. I think it is anyway. She's missing out on so much. She got absolutely no chance of bettering herself."

"She might not want to better herself. She may be perfectly happy with things as they are."

"I know, but I still think it a waste."

"Well I wouldn't worry about it too much. We've got enough problems of our own," her mother replied wearily.

"I suppose so, but…"

"Is tea ready, Mom?" asked Ash as he burst through the kitchen door.

"It'll be another five minutes. You've just got time to wash your hands. And don't leave the towel dirty either. Do it properly!" she answered, dropping the last of the bacon rashers into the sizzling pan.

It took the children only a few minutes to devour their meal, and as they were mopping up the last of the bacon fat with pieces of bread, Ash asked if it was all right for them to go out.

"When you've helped me with the washing up," their mother replied.

"Where are you going anyway?" she asked when they had finished. "I don't want you going down by the brook again and coming back soaked through."

"No, we're not. We're going to the allotments. See who's there," replied Violet.

"All right. Off you go, but mind what you get up to. And don't be too long. There's still the hens to see to."

"I wonder what those two are up to now," mused Claire. "I wish I had their energy though. All I want to do is put my feet up and rest."

Violet and Ash walked down Whispering Lane: the track that led past Ivy Cottage to the allotments. No one knew for sure how the narrow track had come by its name, but it could well have been due to the small spring that rose close by. A little stream flowed from it alongside the lane and the sound it made as it did so might seem, to some, like hushed voices.

"Are you sure he's not here?" asked Ash nervously as they neared Ivy Cottage.

"I saw him go off, heading towards the Crystal Ball earlier. He won't be back for ages."

"How do you know?"

"Because he never gets back till after the pub shuts."

The little black Austin Seven was parked in its usual place on a patch of waste ground between the garage and Ivy Cottage. They stopped and looked around. There was no one else in sight, and all the curtains in Ivy Cottage were, as usual, drawn shut, making it look as though it was deserted.

"I'll keep watch while you go and have a look," Ash whispered.

Violet hesitated. She knew that it was she who was taking the greater risk, and now that it came to it, she almost turned back.

"Go on before somebody comes," Ash urged. "If somebody comes, I'll whistle, and you can hide behind the car."

"Then what? You can't just stand there whistling."

"I'll walk on down to the allotments and come back as soon as it's safe."

"All right then. Keep your eyes open."

She took a deep breath and walked across the waste ground to the car.

Shading her eyes, she peered through the dusty front window, and seeing nothing suspicious there, she moved to the back windows.

Meanwhile, Ash was keeping watch for anyone coming along the path. All of a sudden, a Thrush flew past carrying something in its beak and shot into the hedge nearby. He heard a faint chirping and guessed there was a nest that he had somehow overlooked. He imagined he knew every nest along that stretch of hedgerow: The Blackbird's, Bullfinch's, Wren's and Hedge Sparrow's. He had found them all. He would just take a quick look at this one.

Violet stood on tiptoe to get a better look. The back seat was covered in rubbish. There were old newspapers, empty beer bottles and cigarette packets, a pair of boot and dirty overalls heaped across the seat.

She was about to give up when she spotted a crumpled piece of paper. She could just make out the words: 'Ludlow Livestock Market'.

She put her hand on the door handle and pressed it downwards.

"Hello. Are you looking for something?" a voice suddenly asked.

Violet froze in horror.

"Er, yes. It's a thrush's nest," she heard her brother answer.

She peeped over the car's bonnet to see Ash pointing to a spot in the hedge at the side of the path, and the vicar looking on with interest.

"Ah yes," he said. "Five fledglings, I believe. They should be leaving the nest any day now. I've been keeping an eye on it since she started nest building. This particular pair have held this territory for the two years. Last year, they only managed to rear three young. Still, that's not a bad average."

Ash stared open-mouthed for a second. Adults didn't usually take much notice of birds, or their nests, in his experience, but the vicar seemed to know more than he did.

"I bet you don't know where there's a sparrow hawk's nest," he eventually said.

"I only know of one in *this* area," the vicar answered. "In a stand of Scots pine on the way towards Penny Heath. Now, the interesting thing about the Sparrow Hawk is that when… Oh hello, Violet. I didn't see you there."

Violet had emerged from her hiding place unnoticed and appeared silently as the vicar was warming to his subject.

"Hello, Mr Wren."

"I was just telling your brother an interesting fact about the Sparrow Hawk."

"He's mad on birds, aren't you, Ash? Can't think about anything else sometimes," Violet replied.

Ash squirmed inwardly at this barbed comment.

"Oh well, that's no bad thing… in a boy, of course. So long as it doesn't become an obsession, as it can do so easily," the vicar responded.

"What's an obsession?" ash enquired.

"Something that occupies too much of a person's time and energy," he answered.

"Now, I must be on my way. I'm in search of the elusive pied flycatcher, you know. They should have arrived back weeks ago, but as yet, I haven't spotted one."

"I know where there's a nest," said Ash proudly. "I'll show you if you like."

"That would be splendid," replied the vicar.

"Not right now though," said Violet. "We've got to go to the allotments and then it will be time to go home, wont it, Ash?"

"Oh, that's quite alright. Don't let me detain you. Perhaps, you could show me the nest another day."

As they were about to leave, a thought occurred to Violet.

"Vicar? Can I ask you something?" she said.

"Yes. Of course, what is it?"

"You know how rationing means we should all get enough food and things? Well, say if someone was cheating. Would that be against the law?"

"Well, that would depend. What precisely do you mean by cheating?"

"If a person was keeping lots of food to themselves and hiding it from everybody else, so they had more than they should."

"Mm. Well, that would rather depend on the circumstances; the, err, quantity of food and so on. It would be morally wrong of course, and stockpiling food, petrol and so on is strictly regulated and it would *definitely* be a crime if the items had been bought on the black market, but I don't believe anyone in this parish would do such a thing, so I wouldn't let it concern you. Why do you ask?"

"Oh, it's nothing really, just a story I've been reading."

"But still, these things do happen from time to time. Human nature is very frail, you know. It's easy to succumb to temptation when everything is in such short supply," the vicar said, shaking his head sadly.

"Thank you, Mr Wren. I won't worry about it now," Violet said, giving him a reassuring smile.

Chapter 11

During the next two weeks, Violet kept watch from her bedroom window, which overlooked the garage and gave a tantalising glimpse of Ivy Cottage just beyond. Whenever she could, she would disappear to her room and patiently sit waiting for something to happen. She kept notes in a special notebook with the heading 'Suspect's Movements Log' printed on the cover. Gradually, she built up a list of dates and times of Albert Skinner's comings and goings. Not certain if they would ever lead to anything, but determined to do her best to prove his guilt. She kept the notebook hidden under a loose floorboard.

"What are you doing up there?" her mother called up the stairs, one sunny afternoon. "Why don't you go out and play?"

"I'm writing," she answered, truthfully. "It's too hot outside."

Beryl Sinton considered this response. She was increasingly worried about her daughter, who, she felt, was suffering in her own way more than any of them since her father's disappearance.

"Well, don't stay up there too long. I've just taken a jam sponge cake out of the oven."

Violet appeared almost immediately.

"You and Ash don't seem to be spending much time together lately," her mother said as they sat at the kitchen table.

"Well, he's got other things to do, and I don't always want to be with him and his friends. I'd rather be by myself sometimes."

Ash was in fact spending more time with his friends, and it seemed to his mother that he only came in to eat and sleep now.

74

Claire was working hard on the farm, and to Ash's amazement, she was not thinking of giving up. In fact, she seemed to be enjoying it and was more cheerful than she had been for some time.

"I feel that I'm doing something worthwhile; even if it's only field work," she explained to her mother. "And another thing is that I've been helping Florence with her reading and writing during our lunch breaks. She really is very bright. I think I might even go over to the campsite one of these evenings to give her a bit of extra help."

Florence had indeed been getting some instruction from Claire, and, to her surprise, was finding it quite enjoyable, and was only too happy to agree when Claire suggested she could take her one or two books over to the caravan one evening so that she would have something to read other than the newspapers that they had been reading from at work.

The news had been nearly all about the progress of the war of course, and how the British and American troops were confident that they would soon have the Nazis in retreat. Everyone knew that would require an invasion of mainland Europe, but when and where that would happen was a closely guarded secret.

At Phoenix Farm, Salvo had been busy overhauling the horse-drawn mowing machine and sharpening scythes in preparation for hay making.

Everywhere, people were looking to the skies hoping that the good weather would hold. Rain and wind now could ruin the most carefully laid plans.

That evening, Claire walked to the campsite carrying a book that she thought would be suitable for Florence to read in what little spare time she had. She had chosen it carefully. It needed to be interesting and at the same time challenging enough to further Florence's ability. Eventually, she settled on Heidi: a story about a young girl who goes to live with her grandfather high in the mountains of Switzerland.

When she arrived at the encampment, Florence was sitting with her grandparents on the log seat next to the caravan. She was reading to them from a newspaper, and Claire heard something about Rome. Salvo was there as well, listening to what the newspaper reports had to say. Florence spoke slowly but surely with only a little hesitation at some of the more unfamiliar words.

Florence stopped reading when she saw Claire approaching.

"No, don't stop. That's today's paper, isn't it? I haven't read it yet. What does it say about Italy?" her visitor asked eagerly.

"The Allied Forces have finally liberated Rome, and what is left of the German army is in full retreat northwards. It is expected that –"

She was cut short by Salvo's huge cry of delight.

"Mama Mia! Is fantastic. I can't believe! Is 'appiest day of my life!" he cried, and without another thought, he took Claire in his arms and swung her round and round.

"Sorry. I am carried off," he said, put her down and stepped back apologetically.

"Carried away," Claire laughed. "Don't apologise. I'm happy too. It's great news. What else does it say, Florence?" Claire said, somewhat flustered.

Florence continued to read the rest of the article, describing how the battle had been won, and as she did so, Claire wondered if at last her Father's fate would soon become known. Surely, now it was only a matter of time before the war ended and all the dead and missing were accounted for.

Salvo caught her eye and gave a small apologetic shrug. Claire rolled her eyes.

"We go to the Crystal Ball Sunday? Big celebration, yes?" Salvo asked Herby.

"Oh arr. If this ain't cause for a celebration I don't know what is!" he replied enthusiastically.

"I 'ave to go now. See you Sunday," said Salvo mounting his bike and peddling away with a cheery wave.

"Well we're 'owin' you for teachin' our granddaughter 'ow to read so good aint we 'Erby?" Gran said turning to. her husband.

"We are, right enough. We must give you summat in return," he answered.

"I don't want anything. I've enjoyed doing it."

"No. I won't 'ear of it. We must give you somethin'," Gran insisted.

"I know. Would you tell my fortune for me?"

"Course I will. When would you like me to give you a reading? We could do it now if you want."

"No, I've got to get back, but I could come tomorrow morning. About eleven if that's alright with you."

"Tomorrow morning it is then," said Gran.

"Great. Well, I must be off now. I hope you enjoy the book, Florence."

"Thanks, Claire. I think I will," she said looking up from the book, which already lay open on her lap.

"Well, no one needed to be a fortune teller to see *that* coming," Gran said, when she and Herby were alone.

"What?""Claire and Salvo, of course."

" Don't you go sayin' anythin' though," she quickly added.

"What d'you take me for?" he replied in an offended tone.

"Do you really want me to answer that?" she asked. "Keep it under your trilby 'at or you'll 'ave me to deal with."

"I can keep a secret. Don't you worry about that," Herby replied firmly.

Chapter 12

One Saturday morning, bright and early, Ash set off to meet Frank and Freddy on their family allotment. As he reached Albert Skinner's house, he saw the heavy curtains were as ever drawn across the grimy windows, shutting out the sunlight.

Next to the house was a low brick wall surrounding a small yard with a pigsty in the far corner. The pig was dozing with its snout sticking out of the doorway when it heard Ash approaching. It heaved itself up onto its stubby legs and trotted across the yard. It remembered Ash from when he had thrown it some cabbage stalks a couple of weeks earlier and hoped he might have brought something else to eat.

"Sorry. Nothing for you today," said the boy as he leaned over the wall and scratched the pig's bristly back.

The pig grunted contentedly. Having a good scratch was the next best thing to having something to eat.

"Oi! Watcha think you're doin'?" a voice shouted angrily. "Clear off! Leave my pig alone!" Ash jumped with surprise, and turned to see Albert Skinner standing in his doorway with a walking stick raised threateningly.

"I was only..." Ash began.

"I know you kids. You're all the same. Up to no good. Clear off before I give you what for!" the old man growled as he advanced down his garden path with the heavy stick raised over his head.

Ash decided that reasoning was not going to get him anywhere and backed away, then marched off with as much dignity as he could manage as the angry pig owner broke into a fit of hoarse coughing.

Albert Skinner watched until Ash was out of sight, then turned to go back inside. Another spasm of coughing stopped him in his tracks. He spat into the dirt, then gathered himself together, stepped inside and slammed the door behind him.

Frank and Freddy were already at work on the allotment when Ash arrived a few minutes later still feeling shocked by the unjustified behaviour of the Air Raid Warden.

"Hallo, young Ashford. Come to take my two lads off, have you?" asked Gertie Turner as she dropped a heavy bale of straw at her feet. You'll 'ave to wait while they finish puttin' this straw round the strawberries."

"Can I help?" Ash offered.

"Oh, bless you. Many 'ands make light work as they say."

"We've not got much left to do," said Freddy as they spread the dry straw under the strawberry flowers.

"Been 'ere since six," said Frank.

"Did you see Albert Skinner when you came past Ivy Cottage?" asked Ash.

"No. Too early for him to be about. Why?"

He proceeded to tell them about his confrontation with the Air Raid Warden.

"He's not right in the 'ead. Never as bin. But 'e ull get is come-uppance one of these days," said the twins ' mother as she straightened up and leaned back with her hands on her ample hips.

"Ooh. I'm getting to old fer this," she groaned. "How's your ma getting on these days?"

Ash shrugged. "She's alright really, but it's just that we still don't know what's happened to our dad," he said kicking half-heartedly at a clump of grass.

"Mm. It's a terrible thing, is war, but don't you get giving up hope. Sometimes no news is good news. Keep your chin up," Gertie Turner replied as she tousled his curly hair.

"Anyway, I think we've finished, so off you go and mind what you get up to!"

"Remember me to your ma," she shouted to Ash as they headed off along the footpath towards Cooper's Mill.

"Guess what I've found!" Ash began as soon as they were out of earshot.

"What?"

"Two empty oil drums!" Ash exclaimed proudly.

"No!" said Frank.

"Where?" asked Freddy.

"In a patch of stingers by the millpond."

"We can build a raft," said Frank.

"A landin' craft!" said Freddy.

"An amphibious vehicle," said Ash.

The news that week had all been about D-day and the newspapers had been full of pictures showing British and American troops pouring off amphibious landing craft and storming up the beaches of Normandy. Two empty oil drums were exactly what they needed to re-enact the battle scenes.

The three friends used the cover of the hedgerows and ditches to protect them from the dive-bombers and snipers who were desperate to stop them from reaching the barrels and were lucky to survive with only a few scratches.

Building the landing craft soon proved to be a more challenging operation than they had expected. They had the oildrums and plenty of old floorboards from the abandoned mill but no tools. As they stood discussing what they needed, Florence suddenly appeared.

"Ello then. What you up to? Buildin' a raft?" she enquired casually.

"A landin' craft if you must know," replied Freddy.

"What are you doin' 'ere anyway, Florence?" asked Frank.

"Do you know each other?" asked Ash.

"Yeah. We seen 'er at the farm," said Freddy.

"How are you goin' to fix the boards onto the barrels?" Florence asked.

"That's secret information," said Frank. "We know what we're doin' though. Don't worry."

"Oh, I'm not worried. It's just that I know where there's some rope that could be useful."

"Where?" the twins asked in unison.

"Secret information, I'm afraid," she replied.

"Look, we'll let you join up if you like," said Freddy.

"I've got more important things to do right now, but if you want some rope, there's some in the old barn. Nobody's usin' it. But don't say I told you."

"Thanks," said Ash. "What are you doing down here anyway?"

"Gran sent me to look for some elderflowers but there don't seem to be any in flower yet."

"I know where there's some up by Avens Wood," said Ash. "I can show you if you want."

"What about the raft?" said Frank.

"Landin craft," Freddy corrected.

"We can't do anything till we've got a hammer and nails and the rope," said Ash. "Let's meet here tomorrow afternoon. 14.00 hours. I'll get the hammer. There's bound to be plenty of old nails lying about in the mill. You two get the rope. Alright?"

"You might need a saw as well," said Florence.

"Come on. I'll show you where there's loads of elderflowers," said Ash as he led the way along a rutted track that joined the road near to the old barn.

They had only gone a hundred yards or so when he turned onto a narrow path that wound up between the apple orchards towards a wooded hill. The path grew steeper until it turned sharply above the last orchard. A sandstone cliff appeared in front of them as they turned the corner. Set into it was an empty doorway and three roughly cut square openings where once proper windows would have looked out across the valley. The remains of a brick chimney followed a crevice in the rock face to the cliff-top, behind which rose a wooded slope sheltering the rock-house from the winds.

The path led to a gateway in a low sandstone wall. The wooden gate lay rotting on the ground. Stepping through the gateway, Florence found herself in a garden but not one that had been tended for a long time. The ground sloped upwards towards the rock house, and the path zig-zagged through clumps of tall foxgloves, brambles and gorse bushes, until it levelled out in front of the doorway. The door had long since disappeared leaving just the remains of the wooden door-frame surrounding the gaping entrance. On either side, elder-flower trees had grown up in the sunny shelter of the rock face. They were covered in creamy white flower heads that filled the air with a delicate perfume.

Florence turned and shaded her eyes to look back. From where she stood, the whole of the valley lay spread out below. The Sytch brook meandered through orchards, hop fields and grassy meadows on its way to join the River Teme. Cows and sheep sheltered in the shade of trees and hedges. There were farmyards and barns and the hop kilns with their peculiar con-ical roofs. Where the winding, tree-lined lanes converged at Sytchford, the wooden church spire pointed up towards a cloudless blue sky.

"This is amazing!" she said. "Imagine living 'ere."

"There's a well over there by that old damson tree," Ash replied.

"Let's go and have a look," she said, already picking her way between the gorse bushes.

The well had been topped with cast iron pump and to Flor-ence's surprise, water began to gush from the spout as she pumped the rusty handle. She put her hand under the flow and found that the cold water ran clear.

"Someone's bin usin' this," she said.

"Nobody ever comes up here 'cept me and the twins, and we haven't been for ages," Ash replied.

Florence tasted the water.

"It's good. Tastes fresh," she said thoughtfully.

"Do you want to have a look inside?"

"Yes. Course I do," she answered eagerly.

"I wonder what happened to the people who lived here. Why did they leave?" Florence whispered as they explored the cool, dark rooms cut out of the solid rock.

"I 'spect they found somewhere better to live. It is just a cave after all," Ash replied

"Well, I wouldn't mind livin' 'ere. I think it's great," she said. "I'd better get the elderflowers," she said, suddenly re-membering why they had come.

They went outside into the bright sunlight.

Someone had balanced a wooden plank across two piles of bricks to make a bench under the windows and while Ash sat there, Florence stood in front of one of the bushy trees and whispered something. Then she picked some flowers and put them into her shoulder bag. When the bag was full, she said something else he could not quite hear. Then she came over and sat down next to him.

She noticed there were a few cigarette ends lying in the dust. One had a smear of lipstick on it: a shade of red that looked familiar.

"What were you whispering about just then?" Ash asked.

"I was just letting the elders know what I needed."

Ash's mouth fell open, "You're joking, aren't you?"

"No. You've got to be careful with elders. It's bad luck otherwise. I thought everybody knew that."

Ash could see by the candid expression in her dark eyes that she was telling the truth.

"That's weird. Trees can't hear," he scoffed.

"They can so."

"How?"

"They feel the vibrations. Sound is only vibrations, Ash. Don't they teach you anything at school? Anyway, it shows respect. Gran says every living thing is entitled to respect."

Ash sat and turned these thoughts over in his head.

Florence moved closer.

"I could tell your fortune if you like," she said.

Ash felt uncomfortable all of a sudden. He didn't know if he wanted his fortune told. He'd never thought about it.

"How do you do it? Don't you need a crystal ball or cards or something?" he asked.

"Gran's been showin' me how to do palm readin'."

Ash looked uncertain.

A wren began to sing in a nearby gorse bush.

"Your big sister's 'avin' 'ers done. Come on. Don't be scared. Give me your 'and!" said the Gypsy girl.

Chapter 13

Meanwhile, Claire was feeling nervous. She'd never thought much about fortune telling and had suggested it on the spur of the moment. Now that she stood at the bottom of the caravan steps, she wished that she hadn't been so hasty.

"Come on in," a voice called from within. "We'll just 'ave a cup a tea before we start, shall we?"

Soon they were seated at a small round table covered by a white embroidered linen tablecloth. In the centre, a single candle burned brightly lighting the space around them while leaving the rest of the room in shadows. They sat within this small circle of light: a young woman, pale and nervous, and an old lady with her hair drawn back into a bun wearing a floral headscarf and gold hooped earrings that glowed in the candlelight.

They sipped their tea and chatted for a while about this and that, then Claire came to the point.

"What I really want to know more than anything is, will our father come home safe?"

"Ah, well, first things first. Let me see your 'ands," replied the Gypsy.

She held out her hands palm upwards and the old lady took them in hers and peered intently at them.

"Just relax. Take a few deep breaths and close your eyes," she said softly.

Claire did as she was instructed, feeling more and more at ease in the dim lighting.

Gran then closed her own eyes and they sat in silence. Time seemed to slow down and Claire couldn't say how long they sat there before the old lady began to speak.

"You've been struggling with yourself lately."

Claire gave a start at the sound of the voice.

"There's a man in your life. Someone who you 'ave strong feelin's about. A difficult situation right enough, but just be patient and things will work out for you."

"What about my Dad? Will we ever see him again?" Claire asked anxiously.

"I see a reunion, and quite soon," the old lady answered without hesitation.

"When?"

"Oh, I can't say exactly, but I can tell you that he *is* going to come 'ome one day."

When the reading was finished, Claire felt as though a weight had been lifted from her shoulders.

"Thank you so much. I'm really glad I came to see you," she began. "I don't want you to think I'm interfering, but I'd like to help Florence more. Will you let me see if I can get her into the village school? I know how difficult it is, what with moving from place to place, but even if she gets a few weeks teaching before you leave, it will be worth it," she argued.

"You don't know what it would be like for 'err. None of the other kids will speak to 'err. She'll be treated like a criminal right from the start. No, I'm sorry, but it would do 'err nothin' but 'arm," Gran insisted.

"Well, what if I was to give her a bit more help? Would you mind?"

The old lady thought for a moment before responding.

"No. So long as you've got the time to spare. We'd be very grateful," she said eventually

"If we arrange a regular time, say early evenings for an hour or so once or twice a week? We can sit outside when the weather's nice. What do you think?"

"Yes. Why not? That's alright with me, but let me speak to Florence, and we'll see what she says."

"That's great. Thank you, Mrs Lovesmith," said Claire. "I must dash; I've got a bus to catch."

"You youngsters are always rushin' about. Off you go. Enjoy the film."

"Yes I hope so. It's…" she burst out laughing when she realised that she had not mentioned going to the pictures.

Gran waved Claire goodbye from the steps of the caravan then swirled her tea cup round and round, threw out the dregs and studied the remaining tea leaves intently. She went inside with a worried shake of her head. What she had seen confirmed what she feared but had not revealed. No point in worrying folk when there was nothin' they could do. She would pray. Not for Claire though but for a younger member of the family.

"Perhaps I need more teachin'," said Florence, as she and Ash passed the allotments on their way back from the Rockhouse.

"I thought you were really good," he replied. "How did you know about me nearly dying of scarlet fever when I was little?"

"Oh, that was easy. It was looking into your future that was hard. I couldn't see anythin' at all."

"Perhaps I haven't got a future."

"Course you 'ave, Ash! It's just me. I'm only learning. Gran would be able to see into your future. It takes years of practice to do that though. Perhaps, Violet would let me try with 'er," she added as they came to Ivy Cottage.

Florence stopped and shuddered as she looked at the house.

"What is it?" asked Ash.

"Who lives there?"

"Albert Skinner. You know. The Air Raid Warden?"

"Oh yes! I should have guessed," she answered.

"He's horrible!" exclaimed Ash.

"'E must be very unhappy."

"He's very miserable if that's what you mean. Come on, let's get back and see if you can do any better looking into Violet's future."

"I can't. I've got to take the elderflowers back before they wilt. But I'm going shopping this afternoon. I could call in on the way. We could all go into the village together."

"Yeah. Good idea." he responded

86

"See you about half past one," said Ash when they got to the end of Whispering Lane. "Come round the back."

"Alright. Bye." replied Florence as they parted company.

"Hello Mom. Where's Violet?" asked Ash as soon as he stepped through the door into the kitchen.

"Upstairs, as usual. Where have you been?"

"On the allotments. Met Frank and Freddy. Mrs Turner says to be remembered to you."

"Mm. Where else have you been?"

"We just went down to Cooper's Mill. Florence turned up looking for elderflowers, so I took her up to Avens Wood rock house to get some. Did you know its bad luck to pick them without asking the tree first?"

"Is that what she told you? Superstitious nonsense!"

"She had a go at telling my fortune, but she's not very good at it yet," he continued ignoring his mother's obvious disapproval.

Just then Claire came in.

"Hello. You'll never guess what I've been doing. I've just had my fortune told!" she said brightly.

"Oh no! Not you as well!" their mother groaned.

Ash raced up the stairs and burst into the bedroom leaving his mother and older sister to argue about the rights and wrongs of fortune telling.

Violet was sitting at her dressing table, writing.

"Guess who I met this morning."

"Florence."

"How did you know? You're not what's-it, are you?"

"Psychic? No. I saw you coming up Whispering Lane together."

"She's calling in on her way to the shops this afternoon. She wondered if you wanted to come with us."

"Yes. I'd like that. What time?"

At half past one, there was a knock on the kitchen door which stood open as usual in the summer and there stood Florence, wearing her smart black shoes and a white blouse with a bright red skirt. Her gold earrings glinted in the sunlight.

"Hello. Come on in, Florence. You do look smart," said Beryl Sinton.

A pair of ankle socks wouldn't go amiss though, she could not help but think.

"Florence is here," she shouted up the stairs, and Ash and Violet rushed down discussing what they were going to spend their pocket money on. Violet hurried across the room and took Florence by the hand.

"Come and look at the chicks," she said. "You won't *believe* how much they've grown."

"Can I do a readin' for you sometime, Violet?" Florence asked as they watched the chicks pecking at the corn that Violet had scattered for them.

"What do you mean?"

"Tell you your fortune. Read your palm. Only I need to practice as much as I can."

"I don't know. I'll have to think about it," Violet replied.

"Come on, let's go to the shops," Ash said impatiently. "We can go to Cooper's Mill later and get on with building the raft."

"You be careful. That mill pool is very deep. I don't like you playing there. It's dangerous," his mother warned.

"We are careful, and anyway, we can swim," replied Ash.

"Well, off you go to the shops or you won't have time to do anything else," she replied with a shake of the head.

"Bye, Mom. Won't be long," they said as they set off.

She watched them walk off chatting animatedly to one another, then turned and went inside.

It's good to see violet coming out of herself, she thought.

Chapter 14

Later that afternoon the friends were all on their way to Cooper's Mill when Violet had an idea.

"Why don't we form a gang?" she said.

"We are a gang, aren't we?" replied Ash.

"Not properly," she answered. "Proper gangs have a name."

"And passwords," added Frank.

"And you have to do something. Pass some sort of test before you can join," said Ash.

"Let's call ourselves 'The Gangsters'," suggested Freddy.

"I don't want to be a gangster!" objected Violet. "We're not criminals. I'd rather –"

"I know!" interrupted Ash. "We'll call ourselves... The Nomads."

"What?" asked Frank and Freddy, together.

"Nomads," he repeated.

"What are Nomads?" asked Florence.

"People that don't live in houses. They have tents and camels and they travel about. Mainly in the deserts and that. You know, like in Laurence of Arabia."

"I'm a nomad already then, aren't I?" Florence said. "I don't live in a house, and we're always moving from one place to the next."

"Who's Laurence of Arabia?" asked Frank.

"It doesn't matter. The thing is nomads go wherever they want. They're free!"

Ash concluded, "Let's vote on it. Hands up all those in favour of 'The Nomads'."

Four hands were immediately raised and Freddy had to go along with the result.

Over the next few days, The Nomads devoted as much time as they could to the task of building the raft.

Violet had not entirely abandoned her mission to unmask the hoarder, but even she soon became so excited by the raft that she put it to the back of her mind and threw herself whole-heartedly into the project.

Florence had to work a few hours most days either at the farm or doing errands for her gran and had agreed to spend an hour every Monday and Wednesday evening having tuition from Claire. The others had school to attend and chores to do, but at every opportunity, they would meet at Cooper's Mill trying out various ways and means of constructing something that might support at least one person without tipping over as soon as they got on to it.

They nailed together some old floorboards from the ruined mill and roped the oil drums to some fence posts that Frank and Freddy had got from their allotment. Then finally, one Friday evening, they nailed the deck onto the posts and it was ready to launch.

"Who's going first?" asked Violet as they stood on the side of the pond looking doubtfully at the raft which sat in the water with only a slight tilt to one side.

No one spoke for a moment.

"Let's draw lots," said Ash.

Florence broke off a length of cow parsley stem and cut it into five pieces. She turned her back and hid them in her fist so that just the tips were showing.

"Whoever gets the shortest piece goes first. Agreed?" she said as she held out her arm towards the others.

One by one, they pulled out their chosen stem.

The gang huddled round in a circle to compare their lots, and it was Freddy's stem that was the shortest.

"Wait a minute," said Violet as he was about to climb aboard. "What are we going to call it?"

"Landin craft don't have names. Just numbers," Freddy replied a little scornfully.

"Give me the pole," he added.

Frank handed him a long straight willow pole and he gingerly stepped onto the raft, which wobbled alarmingly for a moment, as it settled lower in the water.

"Push off," urged Frank, and Freddy gave the pole a hearty shove sending the raft away from the shore and the pole into the muddy bank. As he tried to pull it out, the raft shot away leaving Freddy stretching further and further until he toppled into the water as the raft bobbed up and down on the waves.

He surfaced to howls of laughter from his unsympathetic friends and waded out to the raft, waist deep in water. He threw himself onto the deck and lay there dripping like a sponge while the others cheered his brave effort.

The sounds of cheering and laughter drifted over the allotments, reaching the ears of Gertie and her husband, who were just then watering their runner beans.

"Hark at them kids. They're 'avin the time of their lives!" said Gertie.

"AAGH!" she shrieked as a shower of cold water caught her by surprise. "Right! You've asked for it now, Sam Turner!"

"'Ark at those two," said Frank as shrieks of laughter came from the allotments. They sound like a couple of kids.

Albert Skinner had opened a window to let a little cool air into his stuffy living room but slammed it shut when he heard the noise. He was trying to write a letter and needed to concentrate. He was not used to writing, and the floor was littered with crumpled pieces of paper. Albert licked the end of his pencil and began again.

When Violet and Ash got in later that evening, they were exhausted, wet and very late, so they got a long lecture from their mother, and would have been grounded for a week if she had not been secretly glad that Violet seemed so much happier.

"Where's Claire?" asked Violet

"She's gone for a walk with Helen. You know. The land army girl," their mother replied. "I expect they'll call at the Crystal Ball on their way back."

Helen and Claire were at that moment leaning on the stone parapet of the little bridge over the Sytch.

"What a beautiful evening!" sighed Helen. "Makes me wish summer would never end." She took a final drag on her cigarette and blew a cloud of smoke into the air before flicking the glowing end into the stream where it was extinguished with a tiny hiss. A brown trout rose to investigate the disturbance, and quickly dived away as it spotted the two human shapes silhouetted against the sky.

"Soon be dark," observed Claire. "Not that it gets really dark at this time of year. Still, we'd better be getting back."

"Coming to the pub for one before you turn in?" asked Helen.

"Yes. Why not? We've earned it I'd say."

The Crystal Ball was busy as it usually was at weekends. Albert Skinner and Stanley Evans sat in a corner of the barroom playing crib. Alf Carter was sitting on a bench overlooking the bowling green waiting for Salvo to come back from the bar with his pint.

"Thought you'd got lost!" he joked when Salvo eventually emerged carrying two pints of beer.

"Sorry. Is packed up in there."

"Packed out. Not up," Alf corrected.

"English very 'ard. I will learn though."

They were soon joined by Herby, and Gran, who enjoyed the occasional drop of ale as much as he did. They sipped their beer and watched the bowls match as dusk fell and the air grew gradually cooler. Eventually, Gran said, "It's been a lovely evening, but I'm ready for 'ome. Come on, 'Erbert."

"You comin'?" Herby asked Alf.

"Oh-arr. Time for bed. Got a lot on tomorrow."

As they left, they almost bumped into Claire and Helen.

"You'll have to be quick. They've just called last orders," said Herby to the two girls as they hurried past towards the pub. They spotted Salvo and Alf, and waved briefly before entering the bar.

Meanwhile, Joseph Leonard was leaning on the gate of a field where a chestnut mare cropped the grass with her foal nearby. It was just a few days old and still looked ungainly as it gambolled around on its long wobbly legs, but Joe could already see that it was strong and healthy and with luck, one day, it would grow into a fine Suffolk Punch.

In the fading light of the long summer evening, bats flitted overhead twisting and turning as they hunted for insects and higher in the sky, the swifts were putting on a spectacular performance of flying ability. He watched as the birds screamed through the air. They were flying high. That was a sign of good weather. He was about to set off for home when a hare hopped through the hedge into the lane almost at his feet. It was unaware of his presence and he knew that so long as he stayed still it might not spot him. The hare loped across the lane and disappeared through a gateway into the meadow beyond, where he guessed she might have a young one hidden waiting for its evening feed.

The haymaking was underway and going well. The weather was fine, and the mower hadn't broken down once, thanks to Salvo. The horses had worked tirelessly all day and the mown grass lay drying in long strips across the hay-meadows. If the weather held, it would be dry enough to gather up in a day or two. Then he would need all the help he could get to cart it back to the farmyard and build the hayricks.

He knew he could count on Herby, Helen and Claire (who was proving to be a reliable, hard worker.) Then there was Gertie and Sam, and their twin lads. Salvo would be there, and Florence might help out if her gran didn't need her. It would be hard, thirsty work for everyone involved, but Joe had two huge barrels of cider standing in one of the farm buildings with which to keep the adults refreshed, and there was plenty of elderflower cordial for the youngsters.

He would see if Albert Skinner wanted to earn a few pounds as well. He knew he wasn't everybody's cup of tea, but he still felt a twinge of guilt about the way he had to evict the Air Raid Warden when Lower meadow was ploughed up. Not only that but they had served together in the First World War on the Somme. Joe knew how much the experience had affected his old comrade. Seeing him now, it was hard to believe the miserly skinflint had once been a carefree, friendly young man.

He began to walk back to the farm and as he walked, he thought how much this war was now bringing about changes for everyone.

Both of his daughters had joined the Women's Royal Air Force and were rarely able to get back home.

Two of his farm hands had joined the army at the outbreak of war and both their wives, who had helped out part-time, were working in the munitions factory that had been set up a few miles away at Baggots Wood. And now, the Ministry of Agriculture wanted production to increase again. He could not see how it was possible, but it just had to be done if widespread starvation was to be avoided.

At the vicarage, Clifton Wren was slumped in his armchair feeling all of his sixty-eight years of age. He had spent the afternoon mowing the lawn with his old push mower. The new petrol engine mower was sitting in the garden shed with an empty fuel tank due to the shortage of fuel. He needed a gardener. Someone who could help out one or two days a week, but finding such a person now had proved impossible and so, between them, the Wrens managed the large garden themselves as best they could.

The wireless was on and the newscaster was reporting in tones of great urgency how the invasion of mainland Europe was progressing. The Allied Forces were advancing further into France despite suffering some 'inevitable' losses.

Janet Wren sat absorbed, taking in every detail of what was being said.

"I think the war could well be over sometime next year if these reports are accurate," Janet said as she switched the wireless off.

"I hope so!" replied her husband. "Perhaps, I'll be able to get the petrol mower working again then."

There was a moment's silence.

"I don't believe you just said that!" exclaimed Janet.

"Don't you realise what's happening in the world? Millions of people are being killed. There are millions more homeless, hungry refugees trying to escape the bombs. Whole cities have been destroyed and all you can think about is your precious lawnmower."

The vicar opened his mouth as if to respond but thought better of it as his wife continued.

"Just because we're fortunate enough to live in a quiet peaceful backwater away from things, you can't forget how much people are sacrificing and suffering. Look at Beryl Sinton. She still doesn't know if her husband is alive or dead.

"And you're a vicar! You should be giving the people of this parish some support... guidance. You should be helping in some way, not mithering about your lawn! You're obsessed with it! Honestly! I worry about you sometimes. I really do!"

And with that, she swept out of the room leaving the vicar to reflect on the truth of those harsh words.

Chapter 15

After the church service that Sunday morning the vicar asked Beryl if he could call in on his way home for a chat.

Half an hour later, she answered his knock on the front door.

"I've been meaning to call for a while now but what with one thing and another…" he began.

"Oh, I know how it is. I don't know where the time goes, and you must have so many people to visit," she answered

"The thing is, Mrs Sinton I was talking to your son the other day and we were discussing the local bird-life, and he told me that he knew where there was a nesting pair of pied flycatchers. Well, I was very keen to see this, as you can well imagine… perhaps. Anyway, to cut a long story short, he kindly offered to show me the nest site, and I wondered if maybe we could arrange a suitable, err, convenient, that is to say time?"

"How about this afternoon. Shall we say two o'clock?"

"Excellent. I will call here at two then."

"Ashford *will* be pleased. He told me he had been speaking to you about birds and that he had offered to show you this nest. It will be good for him. He could do with a bit more adult male company what with his father being… away."

"Indeed. There are so many young people these days who lack parental guidance. Not that I mean to say you don't…" the vicar added hastily.

"It's true. This war will have damaging effects in all sorts of ways. I don't think anyone has had time to think about that yet," Beryl replied sadly.

"Anyway, I think it's very kind of you to take an interest in Ashford."

"Oh, please don't thank me, Mrs Sinton. It will be a pleasure. Ash is very knowledgeable about birds as you know."

"Well, yes. I suppose he is really," she replied.

She smiled as she showed the vicar to the front door. She couldn't help but feel just a little proud. After all, if Clifton Wren said her son was knowledgeable then he must be.

Three men were standing around the red sports car on the forecourt of the garage when the vicar emerged from Orchard House: Reg Tolley, Salvatore Bonelli and someone in RAF uniform. He realised that it was Robert Westwood and crossed the road to say hello.

"I'm just back for the weekend," Robert explained.

"How are the ribs now?" enquired the vicar.

"Pretty good. I get the odd twinge now and then but can't complain really."

"And what about your job. How's that going?"

"Oh, fine, but between you and me, I'm sick and tired of the whole horrible business. The sooner the war's finished the happier I'll be! I can't wait to get back to a normal life helping run the estate. You know, I thought it was all a bit of a lark when I first joined up. Not anymore."

"Right then. I reckon we've done everything. Do you want to try 'er out?" said Reg, wiping his hands on an oily rag.

"Can I give you a lift, Reverend?" asked Robert.

"Well, I'm going to visit old Mr Hodgekins over Penny Heath way. I was going to cycle, but if it's not out of your way, then yes, I'd be very grateful."

"Hop in then. Let's see if they've found the problem. She hasn't been running quite right since the engine got flooded in that thunderstorm back in the spring."

The vicar settled himself into the passenger seat as the car glided smoothly away from the forecourt and accelerated past the Crystal Ball heading towards the bridge.

"We'll go the long way round. Take the main road then back along the lanes to Penny Heath. I'd like to see Ernie Hodgekins myself. He used to be gamekeeper on the Westwood Estate before he retired," Robert said.

When the car turned onto the main road, Robert put his foot down and the Morgan responded immediately so that in a matter of seconds the hedgerows became just a blur as they sped past.

The vicar had never travelled so fast in his life. He closed his eyes and gripped the seat in terror; sure, that he was about to meet his maker at any moment.

"Are you alright, Vicar? I'm not going too fast, am I?" said Robert after a while.

"No, I'm getting used to it. It's rather exciting, isn't it?" replied his passenger.

They came to a turning onto a side road that led to a hump-back bridge over the river. The car shot up the slope and became airborne for a second as the road dropped away on the other side of the bridge.

"Oops. Sorry about that. I overdid it a bit there," laughed Robert.

By this time, the vicar had turned a shade pale and was mightily relieved to hear Robert say, "I'll slow down a bit. Never know what's round the next bend."

When they pulled up outside the thatched cottage, Robert Westwood was well pleased.

"I don't know what that Italian chap did, but she's running better than ever," he said.

Ernie Hodgekins was seated on a bench by the front door. He was a small man, and every year it seemed to the vicar that he shrank a little more, so that now, well into his eighties, he resembled some sort of a benevolent goblin. No one knew quite how old he was, and he himself couldn't be certain. The vicar had often thought of checking the parish records but hadn't yet got round to it.

"Why if it ain't Mahster Robert!" he exclaimed when he saw his visitor. "Oi wus only a thinkin' about you t'uther day, and bless my soul, ere you be! And Vicar Wren an all. Come on in. I've got some nice damson wine if you'm thirsty."

They followed the old man into his dimly lit front room where stuffed badgers, foxes, stoats and birds of prey sat on every available shelf. A huge salmon occupied pride of place mounted in a glass case over the fireplace.

The old gamekeeper and Robert chatted about times gone by when shooting parties at the Hall would often bag hundreds of pheasants, partridges and rabbits over the course of a weekend.

The vicar was happy to sit and listen for the most part. He had never approved of the wholesale persecution of the birds of prey that was such a large part of the gamekeeper's duties, but he could not help but be impressed with the old man's knowledge of the countryside and the local history of the area. He was a link to a way of life that was disappearing, and it occurred to Clifton Wren that the stories he was listening to should be recorded before it was too late.

"Where do you want me to drop you?" Robert asked as the two men waved goodbye to their host.

"Back at the vicarage if that's alright," replied the vicar.

A few hair-raising minutes later, the Morgan came to a halt outside the vicarage gates and Clifton Wren got out.

"That was an experience I shall never forget, and one which I hope I never have again. Thank you, Robert," he said.

"How was Ernie?" asked Janet as they sat down to lunch.

"Oh. In top form," the vicar replied. "He and Robert had a really good chat about the old days. Of course, Ernie can recall the time before Robert's grandfather was born. He really is a fascinating character."

"And how is Robert these days?"

"He's changed. Grown up, I suppose. Mind you, he's still reckless once he gets behind the wheel of that car of his. I really thought at one point that I was going to die. We were actually airborne when we went over the hump-backed bridge!" the vicar exclaimed.

"I wonder if he might get back together with Claire Sinton," he added thoughtfully.

"I doubt that somehow," Janet responded without hesitation. "Not if the village rumours are to be believed."

"What rumours?"

"Oh, it's probably nothing. You know how people love to gossip."

"Are you still taking young Ash bird-watching this afternoon?" she asked.

"Well, he's taking me to be honest. He's found a pied fly-catcher's nest and you know I've been trying to build up a record of their distribution."

"You'd better get a move on. You said you'd be there at two, didn't you?" Janet reminded him.

"Goodness. Is that the time? Now, where did I leave my binoculars?"

Meanwhile in Orchard Cottage Violet was preparing for an excursion of her own.

"Now, have you got everything?" asked Beryl Sinton.

"Shopping list?"

"Yes, Mom," replied Violet.

"Purse?"

"Yes, Mom."

"Ration books?"

"Yes, Mom."

"Shopping bags?"

Violet held out the bags for her mother to see.

"Alright. Off you go then, and mind the road."

Just then, there was a knock at the front door.

"That'll be the vicar. Ash! The vicar's here!" she shouted up the stairs.

The pied flycatcher's nest was in a hole in an old oak tree. To get there, they would have to pass by the old barn.

"There was a barn owl roosting in there before the field was ploughed up for spuds," said Ash when they reached the gateway. "I s'pect it's roosting somewhere else now," he added.

They stopped and leaning on the gate, surveyed the rows of potatoes with their fresh green leaves showing out of the tops of earthed-up ridges.

"It's such a shame the old meadow had to be ploughed up. Poor old Albert Skinner had to sell off all his ewes and lambs as well," the vicar observed sadly. "But there we are. There

100

are millions of people who need food, and the Ministry of Agriculture has to organise things for the best. I suppose it's a price we have to pay. Perhaps one day it will be returned to meadowland," he concluded hopefully, as they turned and went on their way.

"I thought Mr Leonard owned the field," Ash said casually.

"He does, but he rented it out to Albert until he was instructed to plough it up."

"What if he said no? Just refused to do it?"

"The ministry could have turned him off and handed it over to someone else," the vicar replied. "He really didn't have a choice."

By the time they reached the wood, Ash had begun to worry that they might be too late. "They might have flown," he said. "I think they were about ten-days-old when I saw them last week."

They were, however, just in time. The parents were darting backwards and forwards with beaks full of insects, trying to satisfy their hungry chicks, who the vicar could see would be leaving the nest any day now. The parent birds only got as far as the nest hole where they would be met by one or other of the chicks demanding to be fed.

The vicar passed Ash his binoculars and showed him how to focus them. He was amazed at how close the nest hole seemed and how much detail he could now see.

"I'm going to save up my pocket money and buy some binoculars," he declared as they made their way back.

"Well, you might as well keep these," replied the vicar. "They're an old pair. Perfectly adequate though. I've got better ones somewhere. I just couldn't lay my hands on them before I came out."

On her way to the shops, Violet met up with Florence, who was waiting for her outside the butcher's.

"Where's Ash?" asked Florence casually as they walked towards Mrs Evans' grocery shop.

Violet explained about the vicar and the pied flycatcher.

"Blimey. He was goin' on about flycatcher's weeks ago. The day after I arrived. When you were havin' trouble with those lads."

"Well. He's doing some sort of study on them and Ash knows pretty much everything to do with birds round here, so he's helping him. It keeps him out of trouble, Mom says."

"Have you got much to get?" asked Florence

"I need to get some potatoes from the green-grocer's first," she said checking her shopping list.

Meanwhile, in the grocery store, Mrs Evans was serving Mrs Little, one of her regular customers, who had just called in on the off chance that there might be some butter to be had.

"Margarine, yes. Butter, no," was the disappointing answer to her request.

"It's the war. Rationing. Shortages. I don't know where it will end. And what's it all for?" she continued sourly.

"I don't know," said Mrs Little vaguely.

Mrs Evans leaned forward, rested her folded arms on the counter and looked around the otherwise empty shop.

"You won't believe this," she said.

Mrs Little's eyes widened enquiringly as she moved closer.

That Italian POW came in on Friday. Him and Herby Lovesmith.

"He asked me if I'd got any olive oil. Well, I thought he must have wanted it to get rid of earwax, but he said 'No. I want it for cooking with!'"

Mrs Little pulled a face that expressed both disgust and disbelief.

"But that's not all. He asked me if I'd got any spaghetti! *Spaghetti*, if you please!"

"Spaghetti? Where's he think this is? Athens?" exclaimed Mrs Little indignantly.

"It's a sign of the times, I'm afraid. Sytchford's not what it used to be. It's not enough that we're overrun with Gypsies. Now we've got Italians to put up with!"

"I don't know what the world's coming to," Mrs Little sympathised half-heartedly. "I don't suppose you've got any tinned fruit by any chance?"

"And I'll tell you something else," Mrs Evans continued, ignoring Mrs Little's question.

"You'll never guess who he's been seen walking along the river arm in arm with."

"No! Who?" asked Mrs Little excitedly.

At that moment, the doorbell jangled and in came Violet and Florence.

"Come back later this afternoon and I might have had a delivery of what you wanted," the shopkeeper said.

Later that evening, Ash and Violet were in the orchard, shutting up the hens when a song thrush began to sing from the topmost branch of a tall pear tree.

Ash had his binoculars around his neck, of course, and he immediately trained them on the treetop.

"Can I have a look with them?" asked Violet enviously.

"Go on then, but be careful. Here. Let me show you how to focus them."

"Crikey!" she said as the speckled breast of the songbird came into focus. "It's like I could just reach out and touch it."

"Let me have another look!" said Ash impatiently.

"Wait a minute!" replied Violet as he grabbed hold of the binoculars.

"No arguing, you two," called Claire from the garden as she made her way to the gate.

"Where are you going?" asked Violet.

"To meet Helen, if it's any of your business," she replied cheerfully.

"Bye then," Violet called.

"The vicar told me somethin' interestin' about Albert Skinner this afternoon," Ash said as the gate clanged shut.

"What?" asked Violet, handing the binoculars back.

"Those were his sheep in Lower Meadow. He had to get rid of them so it could be ploughed up."

"So it *was* him in the old barn!" exclaimed Violet excitedly. "I knew it was!"

Chapter 16

Summer solstice was now fast-approaching. The days grew ever longer and the sky was still light well after the children went reluctantly to bed. The hedgerows were full of dog roses and honeysuckle, and foxgloves grew in abundance along the lanes where cow parsley had flowered a few weeks earlier. The meadows had all been mown and two big haystacks stood close by Phoenix Farm.

By this time, the raft was beginning to tilt more and more to one side, and the planks were coming alarmingly loose as the ropes stretched, but somehow it was still afloat. At times, it had suffered bombardments when clods of earth were hurled at it by the defending army on one side of the millpond as the attackers attempted to cross from the other shore. There had been plenty of soakings and a few bruises but otherwise, no one had been injured during these battles. Eventually, though, the novelty began to wear off as gradually, the children found new things to do. Now peace and quiet descended on Cooper's Mill once more, and the raft lay abandoned by the tall reeds growing at the edge of the pond.

The rock house had now become The Nomad's headquarters. They furnished it with old wooden crates and a little kitchen table found in the ruins of the mill house. A battered saucepan and some chipped china cups appeared from the back of a cupboard in Orchard House. They made a fire pit in the garden, close to the doorway, and Florence showed them how to set it up so that they could safely boil up water from the well.

All this was done in utmost secrecy, and they had all sworn an oath never to tell anyone anything about the rock house. The Nomads weren't the only gang of children in

Sytchford and they knew it would not be long before their secret somehow leaked out.

Violet was particularly eager to visit as often she could. She pestered Ash for his binoculars whenever they were there: not to watch birds but to scan the countryside below noting all the landmarks. She had drawn a map of the whole area and another of just the village which she kept with her logbook. When she grew up, she was going to be a spy for the government. Secret Agent Violet Sinton. Only she would need to have a false name of course and learn foreign languages as well. She didn't see any problem with that though.

One day, The Nomads were assembled at the rock house. They were feeling restless, waiting for something to happen. Frank and Freddy began arguing about whether the Spitfire was a better fighter plane than the Hurricane.

"What's that patch of red, I wonder?" Florence asked as she looked out across the valley.

Violet stared to where she was pointing for a moment.

"That's the POW camp at Penny Heath. There's acres of poppies growing round the fence."

Florence shielded her eyes against the sun. "I can't see any buildings," she replied.

"Here. Have a look through these," said Ash, offering her the binoculars.

Florence soon had the camp in focus.

"I can see rows of huts and a fence."

"We can go over one day if you like and have a look. Now that the Italians have been moved out, they're using it for Germans."

"How far away is it?" she asked.

"About five miles. We can take my bike."

"I've never ridden a bike. I can ride a horse though. I'll ride Nelson and you can ride your bike!"

"I'll teach you how to ride a bike. It's easy!" he replied.

"Alright. Do you know how to ride a horse?"

"No."

"Alright. You learn me how… teach me how. Teach me how to ride a bike and *I'll* teach *you* how to ride a horse."

"And me!" exclaimed Violet. "I want to learn as well."

"And me!" the twins chimed in.

So that evening, after tea, they all assembled at the Gypsy campsite, eagerly waiting their first riding lesson.

They watched as Florence rode slowly around showing them how she used the reins and her feet to steer Nelson in the direction she wanted the horse to go.

"Where's the saddle?" asked Violet.

"We haven't got one," was the short answer.

"Red Indians don't have saddles either," said Freddy.

"No. And in the films, they can jump off and on while they're still galloping round the wagon trains," Frank added.

"Well, we're not goin' to try that just yet," Florence said. "Anyway, Nelson isn't likely to break into a trot let alone a gallop!"

Herby and Gran sat and watched from the caravan steps as, one by one, the children were helped up and led round on the patient horse before taking the reins for themselves. They soon discovered that riding a bike was a lot easier than riding a horse; even a well-behaved horse like Nelson.

Frank fell off when attempting to mount and although Freddy managed to stay on, he couldn't persuade Nelson to budge at all. Ash had no more success either. Nelson took no notice of his attempts to steer with reins or feet and headed to the water trough for a drink. Only Violet seemed to find horse riding easy, even managing to get Nelson up to trotting speed while Herby and Gran applauded. Alf Carter had joined them hearing the laughter.

"That was the best evenin's entertainment as we've 'ad for a long time," said Gran as Florence tethered Nelson to a stake in the ground.

"You'm a natural, Violet. I could see you ridin' bareback in the circus," Alf added.

This idea immediately caught her imagination. Perhaps she wouldn't become a secret agent after all. Perhaps she would join the circus instead or why not both? A secret agent pretending to be a circus performer.

"Do you want to help brush him down?" asked Florence, interrupting her thoughts. She did of course and enjoyed it as much as riding.

"I wish we could have a horse," she said wistfully as she brushed Nelson's dusty flanks.

"P'raps you will one day," replied her friend.

When they had finished and Nelson's coat shone, it was time for Florence to have her first cycling lesson.

Ash held onto the saddle while Florence began to find her balance and then gave a final push as she wobbled away on her own. After a few mishaps, she got the hang of it and cycled along confidently as they all made their way back towards the village.

Suddenly, they heard a car approaching and moved to the edge of the narrow road as Evans' grocery van passed heading towards Penny Heath. The van slowed to walking speed as it came level with the children and Stanley Evans raised his hand in greeting. He was holding a cigar between the first two fingers of his chubby hand.

"Thinks he's Winston Churchill, doesn't he?" commented Frank as the van accelerated away.

The children set off again, laughing. They had gone some way before Violet turned to say something to Ash, only to realise that he was still standing looking after the van as it disappeared into the distance.

"Come on, Ash. Hurry up!" she called.

He came running to where they were waiting.

"That was Evans' van we heard when we were hiding in the old barn," he said.

"I knew I'd heard it somewhere before, but I couldn't place it. Then when it drove away just now, I realised that was it."

"Are you sure?" asked Florence.

"Positive. It's the only Morris van around here."

"It's got to be him. Him and Albert Skinner must be in it together," Violet said. "They're selling stuff on the black market! Well, they won't get away with it!"

"What can we do about it?" asked Freddy. "We're not the police."

"Why don't we just report it to the constable?" Ash suggested.

"He wouldn't take any notice of us unless we had some real evidence," replied Violet.

"If we weren't children, it would be different... I know, why not write an anonymous letter? That way, the police wouldn't know we were children."

"If you're going to the law, I don't want anything to do with it," said Florence firmly.

"How about if we can get a look under the counter somehow?" Frank said a little uncertainly.

"What?" Ash responded.

"You know. When stuff's sold on the black market it's always sold under the counter," Frank replied.

"That doesn't mean it's hidden under the counter. Well, not always. It's like saying 'something fell off the back of a lorry' instead of 'it's been stolen'," said Florence.

"I fell off the back of a lorry once," said Freddy. "We wus coming back from pea-picking and I were sitting on top of the load, and the lorry went under some trees and a branch knocked me clean off. It were a good job, the lorry were only going slow and I landed in the hedge, or else I could a bin 'urt good and proper."

"Look, this isn't getting us anywhere. Let's meet tomorrow at the rock house and see if we can think of something," Violet said as they neared the crossroads.

They all agreed to be there at midday before going their separate ways. As things turned out though, their plans had to be put on hold.

Violet developed a sore throat that evening and went to bed with a temperature. Next morning, she felt terrible and came out in a rash of spots. Doctor Grant called and pronounced she had chickenpox and would have to spend, at least, a week in bed and two weeks indoors, away from any other children.

For a few days, Violet lay in bed feeling awful and unable to eat. Then the spots, which had spread from head to foot, began to blister and itch more and more. Scabs formed on the red sores, and it took all of her willpower to stop herself from scratching them. To do so would have left scars when she eventually healed.

Violet felt utterly miserable. Ash was forbidden to go anywhere near her bedroom, and his mother kept a close eye on him for any signs of the illness. Fortunately, none developed, but he was kept off school in case he carried the infection.

Florence delivered a bottle of a salve made up by her Gran and Violet's mother applied it to the itching scabs several times a day. The itching soothed and Violet began to feel better.

Soon, she began to feel bored, and with time on her hands, resumed her watch from her bedroom window. Now though, her surveillance included Evans' Grocery Store and delivery van. Her logbook was filling up with dates and times, comings and goings, and yet none of it seemed to add up to anything that would prove her suspicions.

When the day came that she was allowed out for the first time in nearly three weeks, she was heartily fed up with the whole business. Ash had lost interest but she could never entirely banish the thought that there was a traitor in their midst. One day she would find the truth.

Chapter 17

One Saturday evening, towards the end of July, Violet and Florence were outside the rock house watching Ash fire pebbles from his catapult towards a tin can set on top of the water pump. They were taking turns to see who could hit the rusty target most often. So far, no one had hit it even once.

Ash let out a strangled groan as his shot bounced off the water pump just inches below the tin can.

"Ooh, hard luck! That was close," said Florence. "My turn."

She took the catapult, selected a nice smooth pebble from the path and took careful aim. The can jumped into the air and clattered to the ground as the pebble smacked into it.

"Yes! One to me!" she exclaimed, raising her arms in triumph.

Just then, they heard an owl hooting close by.

Ash cupped his hands around his mouth and replied with an identical call.

It was one of The Nomads' secret signals and it meant Frank and Freddy were on their way.

"Guess what we found?" said Frank when the twins arrived soon after.

"A packet of fags," said Freddy, not giving anybody opportunity to have a guess.

"Woodbines. I've got some matches as well," Frank added proudly.

They all gathered round to examine the cigarette packet.

"Where did you find them?" asked Violet.

"In Whispering Lane, by Ivy Cottage," Freddy replied.

"It was just lyin' there. I thought it was empty, but when I kicked it, I could tell straight away it wasn't," added Frank.

"Bet they're h'Albert Skinner's," said Ash, cruelly mimicking the Air Raid Warden's wheezing speech. "He must have dropped them somehow."

"No. He doesn't smoke tipped cigarettes," said Violet.

"How do you know that?" asked her brother.

"I just do."

"Well, whoever they belonged to they're ours now!" laughed Frank

"Yeah! Finders keepers," said Ash.

"No!"

The others all turned in surprise to look at Violet.

"It's the same as stealing. Like when those horrible bullies tried to keep the sixpence I'd dropped. That's what they said. 'Finders keepers'. "

"That was different," Ash responded. "They knew it was ours. We don't know for sure who dropped these."

"Well, it still doesn't make them ours!" insisted Violet. "I don't know why you want them anyway. Just put them back where you found them."

Ash knew it was futile arguing with his sister when she stood like that with hands on her hips.

"Let's vote on it then," he suggested, knowing full well what the result would be.

"Well, I don't want anything to do with it!" said Violet.

Four Nomads gathered round the fire-pit seated on the logs they had collected during their occupation of the site.

Violet sat alone on the bench with her arms firmly folded and a scowl on her face.

"Any of you smoked before?" asked Florence. The others all shook their heads. She took a cigarette from the pack, placed it between her lips, struck a match and inhaled as she lit up. The others looked on with admiration as she blew the cloud of smoke out expertly.

She passed it on to Freddy, and one by one, they copied her.

Meanwhile, Violet decided that she had no desire to sit and watch her brother and her friends behaving like that. She picked up Ash's binoculars from the bench and wandered over to an outcrop of rock that gave the best views across the valley.

She wasn't looking for anything in particular when Ivy Cottage came into focus. A movement in the lane caught her eye. Someone was crouching low as they moved along the lane past the allotments, keeping close to the hedge. She recognised Albert Skinner.

"He's up to something," she said to herself as she watched him creep towards a gateway where he stopped and raised a hand to shield his eyes from the evening sun. Violet knew that from that spot, there was a clear view of Cooper's Mill.

Albert Skinner nodded in satisfaction. His suspicions had been confirmed. When he had observed Salvatore leaving the allotments and heading to the abandoned mill, he guessed who would be coming to meet him there.

Sure enough, Claire, having parted company with her friend Helen at the garage, walked briskly past Ivy Cottage unaware that she was being watched from behind the dingy curtains. Now that Albert had seen them together, he had all the evidence he needed.

From her vantage point, Violet swung the binoculars to focus on the mill pond. She saw a couple embrace by the edge of the millpond and to her horror, realised who they were.

"Seen anythin' interestin'?" asked Florence, coming up beside her.

As Violet opened her mouth to answer, there was the unmistakeable sound of someone being violently sick. It was Ash.

Florence went over to him and gave him a mug of water.

"Here you are. Drink this. Fags don't suit everybody."

"That just serves you right, Ashford Sinton," scolded Violet as they made their way home.

"I'm never ever smoking another cigarette as long as I live," he replied sheepishly. "You won't let on, will you?"

"Serve you right if I did!"

"Don't grass on 'im," said Florence.

"I won't tell, but he's getting no sympathy from me!" Violet replied.

They had reached the turning for Whispering Lane.

"We've got to water the beans," said Frank.

"Afore it gets too dark," added Freddy.

"I'll come and give you a hand," offered Ash who was already feeling perkier.

"I've got something important to tell you," said Violet when she and Florence were alone.

She didn't really want to tell anyone, but she needed to share her secret with someone, and she was sure she could trust her friend.

"What is it?" asked Florence. "What's the matter?"

"I saw something when we were at the rock house earlier. Somebody. At Cooper's Mill. It was that POW."

"Salvo?"

"He was with Claire, and they were… kissing."

She burst into tears.

Florence was stunned. For once, she was at a loss for words.

"How could she?" wept Violet. "With a rotten murderer like that."

"Salvo's not a murderer, Vi," responded Florence.

"They all are! Germans. Italians. They're all the same. If it wasn't for them, my dad would still be here. He might be dead now!"

Florence wrapped her arms around her friend.

"Don't cry. Come and sit down," she said, leading her by the hand to the war memorial at the crossroads.

They sat side by side on the steps for a while, not speaking until Violet stopped sobbing, blew her nose on a small white handkerchief and smiled weakly at her friend.

"What are you goin' to do?" asked Florence.

"Don't… know," she gulped. "I daren't say anything to Mom. She'd go mad!"

"She would, wouldn't she?" her friend agreed.

"But if I keep it a secret, I'll just be as bad as Claire. Worse! I wish I'd never seen anything. Never picked up those binoculars."

She looked up at her friend imploringly.

"What am I going to do, Florence?"

Florence shrugged helplessly.

"It's difficult. Best not say anythin' just now," she advised. "I'll come over tomorrow evening. We can talk it over then."

"You won't tell anyone, will you?" said Violet anxiously.

"No! 'Course not. You can trust me. See you tomorrow."

Violet went indoors and was about to climb the stairs hoping to postpone speaking to her mother, but just as she put her foot on the bottom step, she was halted by her mother's voice.

"Where have you been till this time, young lady? And where's your brother?"

"Ash's on the allotments with Frank and Freddy. He won't be long," she replied, surprised by the sharpness of her mother's tone.

"Have you seen Claire anywhere? She's supposed to be helping me darn some socks. I don't know what you do to them to wear them out so quickly."

"We can't help it. We don't do it on purpose!" Violet responded crossly.

"Answer me! Have you seen your sister? Yes or no?"

"No. Can I go now?"

"Alright, but don't be up there too long. You can have some toast and marmite for supper," she said in a kindlier voice.

Flipping heck. What's wrong with her? wondered Violet. *It's a good job she doesn't know what I know.*

Salvatore walked back from Cooper's Mill deep in thought after his brief meeting with Claire. They both knew that they were heading for trouble if they continued to see one another. Someone was bound to find out, and then what? He was not concerned for himself but for Claire. She would be the one to bear the full brunt of the repercussions. He decided that for her sake, he would have to end their relationship. He looked up and realised he had arrived at the allotments.

He had taken to helping out on the allotments in his spare time, and eventually, he cleared the brambles from an abandoned plot uncovering a small broken-down glasshouse. He planted it up with tomatoes, which were now growing tall and bearing fruit. He ground out his cigarette and picked up a watering can.

"Want me to help you with anythin'?" Ash enquired eagerly as he appeared from the Turners shed.

"Yes. Thank you. Can you tie tomatoes up to canes for me? Like so?" He pointed to where they had been tied lower down.

Salvatore began picking the red fruits into a basket while Ash tied the vines to their supports. He had come to like the Italian and his naturally friendly easy-going way and despite his mother and young sister's disapproval they got on well together.

"Where in Italy do you live?" he asked.

"I show you."

He took a stick and drew the outline of Italy in the dirt then a cross.

"This is my 'ome. Right 'ere," he said proudly.

"That's in the north, isn't it?"

"Si. In the mountains."

"When the war's over, I s'pose you'll go back to Italy,"

"Yes. Of course. I cannot wait. After a while, I may come back. Is nice 'ere."

"OK. We finish. Is enough for today, I think. You go straight 'ome now. Is getting late."

"Take these for your Mama," he added, handing Ash a few tomatoes wrapped in a rhubarb leaf.

"Thanks. Ciao, Salvo."

"Ciao, Ash."

Ash hurried home thinking his mother would be pleased with the fruit, but he was mistaken.

"What time do you call this?" Ash's mother fired the question at him as soon as he set foot in the kitchen.

"Sorry, Mom. Got waylaid. I've brought some tomatoes back," he replied holding them out proudly.

"Who gave you these?" his mother asked holding the tomatoes at arm's length as though they were unexploded hand grenades.

"Salvo."

"What have I told you about that person?"

"Err."

"I've told you not to have anything to do with him, haven't I?"

"Err. I know, but…"

"No buts. You're not to speak to him. Is that understood?"

"Err. Yes. Sorry. It was just that…"

"I don't want to hear any excuses. Bed for you and no supper!"

"Crikey! What's the matter with her?" thought the crestfallen lad as he trudged upstairs.

Chapter 18

Violet lay awake with the same thoughts and unanswered questions tormenting her again and again.

Should she confront her sister?
Should she tell her mother?
Was there some way that she could get Claire to drop Salvatore without her mother finding out about it?
Or *should she keep quiet and wait for someone else to let the cat out of the bag? After all, if Albert Skinner knew, the whole village would know soon enough.*
But then again, wouldn't it be best for her mother to find out before everyone else?

And was she wise to confide in Florence? The awful thought occurred to her that Florence had known. Claire and Salvatore worked together and so did Florence! And he was always hanging round the Gypsy campsite, and Claire often went there in the evenings to help Florence with her reading and writing. Florence *must* have known something was going on all along. But she'd never let on. This realisation was the worst thing of all.

Finally, through sheer exhaustion, she fell into a fitful sleep as a full moon rose above the village rooftops.

The hens shuffled nervously on their perches in the hen house as a fox sniffed around the wire netting of the pen looking for a weak spot.

The silence was punctuated by a dog barking somewhere in the distance then all fell quiet again.

The back-kitchen door of Orchard House swung open and a white shape emerged into the moonlight.

Ever alert for the slightest sign of danger, the fox froze with one paw raised in the air as the figure floated slowly forwards, then it turned and ran gracefully across the orchard. With a final backwards glance, it disappeared through a hole in the hedge.

Violet, in her nightdress, moved slowly but surely, although her eyes remained closed, along the garden path.

Her mother suddenly woke up feeling that something wasn't right. A breath of cool night air wafted through the kitchen and up the stairs as she got out of bed and instinctively went to check on her children. She found Violet's bed empty.

Her alarm intensified when she discovered the back door wide open, and she struggled to control a sense of rising panic as she searched the shadows for some clue as to which way Violet had gone. To her relief, she saw her sitting on the swing suspended from a branch of the walnut tree that overhung the lawn. Her white nightdress glowed ghostly in the moonlight as she swung to and fro, and as Beryl came closer, she realised her daughter was humming softly to herself.

"Come on. Let's go back to bed now," she said gently laying a hand on Violet's shoulder.

"What am I doing out here on the swing?" Violet asked, looking around at the moonlit garden.

You've been sleepwalking again, that's all. Come on, let's go in. It's getting chilly out here."

Violet had begun to sleepwalk shortly after her father had been reported missing, but it had been several months since the last episode and her mother had hoped she was over it.

Beryl was careful not to wake the others as she put her daughter back to bed. When she was sure that she was safely tucked up and sleeping soundly, she tiptoed downstairs and made herself a cup of tea. She sat at the kitchen table, deep in thought.

Her husband was missing.

Violet was sleepwalking, and Ash was struggling at school.

And Claire, who should be her rock, was instead her biggest worry of all.

She opened her handbag and took out the letter that had arrived that morning. She quickly read it again and put it away. It simply said:

YOU SHOULD KNOW CLAIRE AS BEEN SEEING THE ITALIAN PRISONER OF WAR.
A FREND.

She wondered if it had been written by a child or someone uneducated. The spelling seemed to point to that unless it was meant to mislead. In any event, she didn't believe the content. It was malicious. A poison pen letter. But who would do such a thing? And why? Surely it *couldn't* be true!

She realised there was only one way to find out. She would have to confront her daughter and ask her straight out.

"I didn't think we would find any blackberries yet. It's still too early for them," said Claire as she walked with her mother along Mill Lane later that morning searching the hedgerows where the berries hung unripe in orange and red clusters.

"That's not really why I wanted you to come out with me," Beryl answered, stopping in her tracks.

"This was pushed through the door yesterday," she said taking the letter from her handbag.

Claire read it and handed it back.

"I knew someone would find out. You can't keep anything to yourself in this village."

"So, it is true then?"

"Yes," her daughter sighed, "It is true. We have seen each other once or twice but it's not serious. It's only..."

"How could you? He's a POW for goodness sake!"

"That doesn't mean he's a criminal! He's a good person. He never wanted to be a soldier. We're all on the same side now anyway!"

"Your father didn't want to go to war either, but you seem to have forgotten that he went missing in Italy. *Italy!* Your boyfriend's home!"

119

"I suppose that was why you were so keen on visiting Florence, saying you wanted to help her reading and writing. And I was daft enough to believe you!"

"No! It wasn't like that. I really did want to... *do* want to help her."

"You've deceived me, Claire, and you've betrayed your father as well. Thank God, Violet knows nothing about it. It's got to stop. You know that, don't you?"

"I know, I know. But please don't report him. Mr Leonard needs his help, and I won't be working on the farm after next week. I've already applied for a job at the munitions factory."

This piece of news came as another unwelcome surprise to Beryl Sinton. The munitions factory was a dangerous place to work. Apart from the possibility that it would become the target for enemy bombers, there was also the risk of accidents. Explosions had occurred in other such factories, and although the authorities tried to keep it quiet, everyone knew that lives had been lost.

If that wasn't bad enough, working with nitro-glycerine and other chemicals gave the workers headaches and turned their skin yellow.

"There's no need for that," Beryl sighed.

"I think it's for the best," replied Claire. "It's all arranged anyway."

Chapter 19

That evening, Ash sat on the back-kitchen doorstep busily inflating a brown leather football with a bicycle pump.

The football had lain neglected under his bed all summer. Cricket was the only game the village children thought about during the summer and sheep could often be seen grazing on the football field. But something had changed. When Ash went out to feed the hens that morning, there was mist across the fields and a nip in the air. Summer was coming to an end.

When the ball was inflated to his satisfaction, he had the tricky job of tucking the valve away and lacing it up. He bounced it up and down a few times and satisfied with his efforts, set to work with waterproofing the leather using a tin of dubbin applied with an old shoe brush. Finally, all was ready. All he needed now was someone to play with. He guessed Frank and Freddy would probably be on the allotment and certain to be up for a kick- about, so pulling on his football boots and a thick woollen pullover he headed off in that direction with the football tucked safely under his arm.

When Ash reached the allotments, he was disappointed to find that there was no one there. He decided to go home. Perhaps he could persuade Violet to have a game in the orchard. They could take turns at penalties.

He hadn't gone far however, when he found his path blocked as Nodder Crump, Billy Butcher and Jack Spragg appeared coming his way.

"It's Ash Sinton! Look, he's got a footy! Let's get 'im!" Nodder shouted.

Ash turned and fled.

Claire, meanwhile, was just leaving Orchard House on her way to meet Salvatore on the riverbank below Cooper's Mill.

She could not stop seeing him without saying goodbye, but after this, it would be over.

"Yes. I promise," she said to her mother as she opened the door and stepped out. She walked quickly into high street, past the Crystal Ball towards the bridge. From there, she would take the riverside path towards the mill.

Violet watched from her bedroom window. Earlier, she had observed Salvatore go down Whispering Lane towards the allotments. She guessed her sister was going to meet him somewhere by Cooper's Mill.

She crept downstairs and slipped unnoticed out of the back door determined to follow her sister and confront her. Just as she reached the crossroads, Florence came round the corner.

"Oh, hello Vi. Where are you off to?" Florence enquired.

"Nowhere. Where are you going?" she answered defensively.

"I was coming to see you, like we arranged. That's Claire walking towards the river, isn't it?" she added.

Violet didn't answer.

"You're following her, aren't you?"

"None of your business!"

"Look, I know what you're thinking. You think I knew. You think I didn't tell you and I should have done. Well, you're right. I did know there was something going on, but what could I say?"

"You should have told me. I thought you were my friend."

"How could I? You don't want to tell your ma, do you? You don't want to upset her. Well, that's just the same as me not wanting to upset you. What would be the point? Me and you are both in the same boat, knowing things we didn't want to know."

Violet was in no mood to listen to reason though, and besides, she didn't have time right at that moment.

"I've got to go," she said.

Florence was suddenly overcome with a feeling that all this had happened before, as though she was reliving a dream.

She was certain that something important was going to happen and that she ought to be there when it did.

"Wait. I'm comin' with you!" she heard herself say.

Ash ran as fast as he could in his heavy boots, but his pursuers were bigger, stronger and faster. Gradually, they closed in on him, and when he reached the millpond, he could run no more. He turned gasping for breath as the three jeering youths circled their prey.

He felt a shove in the back and then there was a flurry of pushing and jostling, which ended when he was knocked to the ground and to his dismay, saw his football being booted high into the air and land with a splash in the middle of the pond.

"Wathcha done that for?" demanded Nodder.

"It weren't s'posed to land in the pond," replied Billy, glumly.

"Well, it did! Right in the middle!" said Jack. "Idiot!"

"Who are you callin' an idiot?" demanded Billy aggressively as he pushed Jack in the chest.

Ash looked on as they began arguing amongst themselves. Then much to his relief, they wandered off back towards the village. They seemed to have forgotten about him altogether.

"What's wrong with those idiots?" he wondered as he got slowly to his feet and watched as they disappeared round a bend in the path.

"What makes them behave like that?"

He could not imagine and he didn't have time to waste thinking about it. He had to get his football back. If he didn't, there was no prospect of getting another until Christmas if he was lucky.

That would be halfway through the season. Besides, the football was a birthday present from his dad. He had to get it!

He brushed the dirt off his clothes and winced in pain. His upper arm felt stiff and he guessed he would have an ugly bruise there next morning. Apart from that though, he hadn't come off too badly.

The raft was lying half-submerged against the reeds on the far side of the pond. It was in a sorry state listing to one side and with its deck looking as though it might easily part company with the rusty barrels that had been slowly filling with water ever since the raft was put together.

Searching around in the ruins of the mill, he found a length of rope left over from the raft building and the pole, which was lying in the grass. He made his way round the pond to get as close as he could and after several attempts, finally managed to lasso a piece of timber sticking out of the deck. His arm ached as he pulled the raft free from the reeds, but he persevered, and soon, it bumped against the bank at his feet.

He gingerly climbed aboard and as he did so, the barrels sank deeper into the muddy water. For a moment, he almost abandoned the rescue attempt as the raft rocked alarmingly under his feet and he struggled to keep his balance, but having got this far, he wasn't going to give up now. He gritted his teeth and pushed away from the safety of the bank. The raft bobbed up and down, and something beneath his feet gave way with an ominous crack but somehow it held together and moved slowly into deeper water. Ash polled carefully towards his goal, but each time the raft moved forward, it sent out a bow wave that pushed the football away. Gradually though, he got closer until the ball was in reach but by now, he was right in the middle of the pond. He knelt down and reached out for it, and as he did so, the raft rolled onto its side pitching him head first into the ice-cold water.

He wasn't alarmed, just annoyed as he came to the surface. He realised he should have guessed that would happen as soon as he leaned sideways. He looked around just as the raft sank from view. He tried to swim and found he couldn't move his arm. His clothes were weighing him down. He tried to grab hold of the football, but with only one good arm it kept slipping out of his grasp. He began to feel swamped by a growing panic.

Meanwhile, Salvatore was sitting on a fallen tree trunk by the river, waiting for Claire. The shadows were lengthening, and the trout were rising to snatch tiny insects from the surface of the water. It was such a perfect, peaceful summer evening that Salvatore found it hard to imagine that war was still raging across Europe.

A few days before, he had, finally, received a parcel of letters from home. He took one from his jacket pocket and as he re-read it, he was overcome with a longing to return there. He carefully folded the letter and replaced it in his pocket, then looked to see if there was any sign of Claire. Immediately, he wished he could find a way to stay in Sytchford forever.

"'Ees a war in my 'eart," he said ruefully to himself.

It was then that he heard a desperate cry for help. He knew instinctively that what he had heard was not a children's game. It held a chilling note of terror that could not be ignored, and he found himself running towards the millpond with its echo ringing in his ears.

Ash sank into the cold darkness, his lungs demanding he breathe, but he knew that to try and take a breath would be fatal. He fought with himself not to panic as he descended deeper and deeper. Then his foot came to rest on something flat and solid. He knew at once what it was. The raft had sunk on its side and the barrels had settled, standing upright in the mud. He had a firm platform under his feet, and gathering all his strength, he pushed upwards. He came to the surface and filled his lungs with air with one desperate gasp before the water pulled him back down.

Salvatore was just in time to catch a glimpse of an arm disappearing from view in the centre of an expanding circle of ripples. He threw off his jacket and kicking off his shoes, dived headlong into the pond.

Claire had also heard a faint cry for help and, recognising the voice, had run towards it.

By the time she got to the pond, all she saw was Salvatore's jacket and shoes lying where he had discarded them. Then to her astonishment, the pond erupted as Salvatore came to the surface with one arm supporting Ash's limp body.

He began to swim to shore with his free arm while trying to keep the boy's head above water with the other, but Ash's saturated clothes weighed heavy and it was all Salvatore could do to keep them both afloat. He knew he was losing the struggle.

It was then that Violet and Florence arrived on the scene. Having seen Claire break into a run, they had, at first, exchanged puzzled looks. Then Florence started running and Violet followed.

They saw Salvatore holding Ash and fighting to stay afloat. Claire was wading into the water, which was chest deep, and all three were in danger of drowning. For a moment, they stood transfixed in horror then Florence sprang into action.

The rope had slipped free as the raft sank. She rushed to where one end still lay on the bank and pulled it towards her. She knew she only had time for one throw. It had to be a good one and thankfully, it was: landing with a splash close enough for Salvatore to grab hold of it before it sank. Florence and Violet hauled him to where they stood on dry ground. He staggered from the water and collapsed to his knees laying Ash down on the grass.

"He's not breathing," Claire sobbed as she looked down on the deathly pale seemingly lifeless body.

They all looked on helplessly as Ash's life was slipping away.

"Stand back. Let me get to 'im," said a familiar wheezing voice. They turned at once to see Albert Skinner flicking a cigarette end into the pond.

"'E's not dead. Still got a pulse," he said calmly as he knelt with fingers pressed to the boy's neck. He breathed several times into Ash's mouth. Still, there was no sign of life. Albert Skinner began to press down on Ash's chest. Once, twice, three times, and then Ash coughed, gasped, spluttered and blinked his eyes open. He was still as white as a sheet and Claire was alarmed when he was suddenly sick, but then the colour began to return to his face and a few minutes later, he was sitting up supported by his big sister as Albert Skinner slumped exhausted by his efforts. Claire slipped off her coat and wrapped it around her shivering brother.

"You saved his life. He would have died if you hadn't been here," she said.

"'E saved 'im," he said, jerking his head in the direction of Salvatore. "Best get 'im 'ome to bed anyway afore 'e gets pneumonia."

The effort brought on a bout of coughing which subsided as he lit a cigarette and inhaled gratefully.

"Run on ahead, Violet and tell Mother what's happened. Then get Doctor Grant," urged Claire.

Salvatore lifted Ash into his arms and they set off for Orchard House as the sun descended to the treetops throwing long shadows across their path.

"I'll be sayin' good h'evenin to you anyway," said Albert when they reached Ivy Cottage. "Don't need my 'elp now."

"You're a hero, Mr Skinner," said Claire. "We won't ever forget what you did."

Albert Skinner just shook his head and made a sound that might have been a laugh or just another wheeze as he closed the door behind him.

Salvatore was carrying Ash up to bed when Doctor Grant knocked on the front door.

Violet let him in and the elderly overweight GP stomped up the stairs without further ado.

Beryl and Claire watched on anxiously as he applied the stethoscope to Ash's chest and back.

"How long was he unconscious for?" he enquired as he went about the examination.

"It seemed like ages, but I suppose it must only have been a few seconds after Albert Skinner got to work on him. He was unconscious when they got him to the bank though," Claire said.

"And you say the Italian POW rescued him?"

"He did. But if it hadn't been for Violet's friend Florence, they both would have drowned."

"I ought to take a look at him as well while I'm here," the doctor said.

"Well! He's a very lucky boy, Mrs Sinton. Another minute and he would not be with us now," he concluded placing his stethoscope carefully in his battered leather bag and snapping it shut.

"Will he be alright? Shouldn't he be in hospital?" she asked

"Hospital? Good Lord, No! Rest assured this is the best place for him. With you looking after him, he'll be up and running about in no time. Keep an eye on him. Keep him warm. Plenty of hot drinks. I'll call in again tomorrow. In the meantime, just call me if you're worried about anything."

"And as for you young Ashford, be more careful in the future. Your mother's got enough on her plate without you scaring the living daylights out of her!"

"Now, let's have a look at this Italian chap."

Salvatore was still wearing his soaking wet clothes and was shivering violently as he stood in the kitchen with a pool of water forming around his feet.

"Someone get this man a hot drink," the doctor ordered. "And find him some dry clothes."

Before long, Salvatore was seated in front of the range. He was wearing some of Sidney Sinton's old clothes and cupping a mug of hot tea laced with a good helping of whiskey. The range was throwing out plenty of heat and his shivering had stopped.

Doctor Grant was sitting at the kitchen table with an empty glass in front of him.

Violet was slumped in an armchair looking bemused.

Claire was having a bath and changing into dry clothes.

"Where's Florence?" Beryl asked, suddenly realising that she had not seen her.

"She went home as soon as we'd told Doctor Grant," said Violet.

"I must go and thank her in the morning. She saved two, maybe three lives. If you girls hadn't been there..." she stopped as she wondered to herself. *Why were they there?*

"Would you like another drop of whiskey before you go, doctor?" she asked.

"I would, but I ought to look in on Albert," he replied as he hauled himself to his feet.

"I should go now also," said Salvatore

"Can I give you a lift? Car's just outside. It will only take a few minutes to check on Albert"

"Thank you. I would be glad."

"Will you come back tomorrow? Your clothes will be dry by then."

"Thank you, Mrs Sinton. I will try and come tomorrow evening if it is OK."

"Yes, of course. Come whenever you can."

At that, Claire appeared in the doorway. There was a moment of awkward silence.

"Salvatore is leaving now, Claire," said Beryl. "See him out, will you?"

"We've got a lot to sort out," said her mother when she returned a few minutes later smiling happily. "It will keep till the morning though. We're all exhausted. There is only one thing I need to know before then."

"What were you doing down by the river, Violet?"

Violet shrugged.

"You were following your sister, weren't you?"

"Yes, I was," she replied miserably. "She's been seeing Salvatore. I wanted to tell them to stop before you found out."

"How long have you known?"

"Not long. I couldn't tell you. I wanted to, but I thought you'd be too upset. I didn't know what to do," she sobbed.

"Oh, Violet. Come here," her mother said, pulling her close and wrapping her arms around her daughter.

That night, sleep came quickly to Violet despite her world having been turned upside down.

Chapter 20

Next morning, Ash was sitting up in bed and tucking into a boiled egg and toasted soldiers when Violet was allowed in to see him.

When he had finished, she carried the tray of breakfast things downstairs.

"Don't stay there bothering him too long. Let him rest," her mother called as she hurried back to sit on the end of the bed.

"What happened?" she asked.

"I don't know. I was trying to reach my football. I remember getting on the raft. I can't remember anything then till I woke up soaking wet with everybody looking at me."

"Why was the football in the pond?"

"Nodder and his mates took it off me. One of them booted it into the pond. They thought it was funny."

"They would!"

"I must have fallen off the raft, I suppose."

"I think it must have sunk. I didn't see it when we got you out."

"Why were you there?" Ash asked. "And Salvatore? And Claire?"

"Listen. I'll tell you everything."

"It started when I found out about Claire and Salvatore."

"What about them?"

"They were seeing one another."

"Of course, they were. They saw each other every day on the farm."

"Not like that."

"You mean…?"

"Yes! Honestly, Ash, you can be so dim sometimes!"

"So, what I don't understand is what was Albert Skinner doing there?" Ash asked when Violet had finished recounting the rescue.

"He was spying on Claire. He must have heard you shouting."

"Come on down now, Violet. Doctor Grant will be here soon," her mother called.

"I'll come back up later," she said as she left the bedroom.

Salvo was drowning. A giant octopus was pulling him down into the darkness, and the more he struggled to get free the more tightly its tentacles held him captive. He cried out for help and the sound of his own voice woke him from his nightmare. He sat up and untangled himself from the blanket in the darkness of the bunkhouse. Dawn was just beginning to lighten the horizon and the farmyard cock stretched out its neck and called a defiant challenge to greet the new day. Salvo heaved a sigh of relief at the familiar sound and his heart rate gradually slowed. Many times, he had cursed the bird for disturbing his sleep so early, but this morning, he felt grateful. He was alive!

The smell of bacon and eggs frying in the pan wafted through the farmhouse kitchen window as he stood in the yard pumping cold water into a tin basin. As soon as he had washed, he crossed the farmyard and knocked on the door, hoping that there might be a sausage to go with the bacon and eggs this morning. He felt as though he had not eaten for a week.

"Is it right what they're saying? It was you that saved young Ash from drowning yesterday?" enquired Bryony when she opened the farmhouse door.

"Yes, but I am not the only one."

"Come on in."

"Now sit down and tell us all about it," she prompted as she set three mugs of tea out on the kitchen table.

"Well. Is like this. I was walkin' along the river near Cooper's Mill last evenin' and…"

"On your way to meet Claire Sinton," Bryony interjected giving him a sideways look.

"'Ow you know that?"

131

"That's what we heard."

"OK. Is true. So I wait where we gonna meet, and I 'ear a child shout ''Elp! 'Elp!' I know it is not a game. Is really serious. So, I run to see what is 'appenin' and when I get to the pond, I see someone's arm disappear under the water. I swim pretty good so I jump in a water and swim out to where 'e go down. I feel around and I am lucky. I find 'im quick. But Ash is so 'eavy. I think 'Oh no! You gonna drown Salvo if you don't let 'im go!'"

Bryony and Joe listened in silence as Salvo continued.

He gave them the full story, hardly pausing for breath right up until the moment he left Orchard House with Doctor Grant, then added:

"What I don't understand is 'ow they all come there, and 'ow Albert Skinner knew what to do."

"I don't know why he was there, but I'm not surprised he knew how to save Ash's life," Joe said as he gently guided a hen out of the door with the tea tray.

"He was in the medical corps during the Great War," he continued as he sat down. "He was one of the people who went out to bring back the dead and injured from the battlefields on stretchers. First aid. Resuscitation. He did it every night and day. Usually with bullets and shrapnel flying round as well. Saved god knows how many lives out there."

Anyway, one night he was out in no-man's land looking for someone who was shouting for help. There was a gas attack and he got caught in it. He managed to make it back to the trenches but he was never the same again. He lost his marbles for a while."

"Marbles?"

Joe pointed to his head and made a stirring movement.

"Ah. Crazy."

"Well, anyway, he spent a long time in hospital."

"It's a wonder he's still alive," added Bryony.

"And always 'e 'as a cigarette. That cannot be good for 'im," said Salvo.

"He says they keep him alive. They make him cough and that clears his lungs he reckons," replied Joe.

"Is a joke, yes?"

"No. He really and truly believes that smoking is good for him," replied Bryony.

"In that case, I think 'e is *still* crazy!" Salvo laughed.

Chapter 21

Crazy or not, Albert Skinner was a sick man.

Doctor Grant closed the door quietly as he left Ivy Cottage wondering how long it would be before his patient would have to be admitted to the hospital. He would have no choice if his condition worsened, of that he was certain.

His next call was at Orchard House. He examined Ash and was pleased to find there was no sign of any fluid in the lungs.

"Everything sounds as it should, Mrs Sinton. He can get up for a while this evening. It will do him good to have a bit of exercise so long as he doesn't overdo it."

"Thank you, doctor. That's a relief. You'll send me the bill, won't you?"

"No. There won't be any charge. I haven't done anything except look at him."

"Well, at least take some eggs," Beryl replied. "You must have something for your trouble."

"It's been no trouble, but I won't say no. That's very much appreciated. Thank you."

"You've been to see Albert Skinner, I think. How is he?"

"To tell you the truth, he should be in the hospital. His breathing is really bad, and he's not eating properly. I'm worried that he could develop pneumonia in that damp cold house, but he won't have it. He says he can't leave his pig."

"Do you think he would agree to have some help? It's only over the road. We owe him such a lot."

"You can only try, but you know what he's like. He never lets anyone in if he can help it. He wouldn't let me in if he wasn't so ill."

"Well, I'll take him some soup at lunchtime and see if I can do anything to help," Beryl insisted.

As soon as the doctor was through the door, she began issuing instructions.

"Violet, go and find a handful of parsley, some mint, green beans and a couple of those nice tomatoes."

"Claire, can you dice some potatoes and chop a stick of celery very fine? If you get the soup on the go, I'll get on with the washing."

Soon, the soup was simmering away on the range. Claire added seasoning, gave it a stir and placed the lid back on the saucepan leaving a gap where steam escaped along with the sweet aromas of the fresh vegetables and herbs.

"Keep an eye on the soup please, Violet. I'm going to help with the wash," she said when she was satisfied with everything.

The wash house stood outside, conveniently near the kitchen door. It was built like a miniature house with a window, door and chimney. Inside, there was a brick fireplace with a big old copper bowl built in above and a wooden dolly tub, a mangle, an earthenware sink and wooden draining board. Above the sink, a brass tap provided all the cold water that was needed.

Beryl had filled the boiler and lit the fire first thing so now; the little room was full of steam that condensed on the cold red brick floor which would have been slippery were it not for herringbone pattern moulded into the bricks. She had nearly finished washing Salvatore's jacket and trousers when Claire came to help. Together, they lifted them out of the tub and wrung them out. Then they rinsed them in the sink before wringing them out again. Finally, Beryl fed the clothing into the rollers as Claire turned the handle at the side of the mangle, and the damp clothes dropped into the wash basket ready to be pegged out on the line.

Beryl picked up the jacket from the wash basket to shake out some of the creases. She held it out in front of her and shook her head.

"This won't do," she said.

"Oh no! What's wrong?" asked Claire

"These red patches. Fetch me some scissors and I'll un-pick the stitching and get them off."

Florence arrived as Beryl and Claire were preparing to leave for Ivy Cottage. She appeared at the back-kitchen door holding a small green bottle with a cork stopper.

"Oh, hello, Florence. Come on in," said Claire, seeing her hovering uncertainly on the doorstep. "What have you got there?"

"Gran sent this for Mr Skinner. It's good for anything to do with the lungs. She wondered if you'd mind giving it to him."

"Yes, of course. We're just on our way there."

"I've written the instructions on the label," said Florence, handing the bottle to Beryl.

"Violet! Florence is here!" Claire shouted up the stairs.

"We can never repay what you did yesterday," said Beryl, placing a hand on Florence's shoulder. "If it hadn't been for your quick thinking, I don't like to think what would have happened."

"I only helped. It was Salvo and Mr Skinner who saved him," she replied.

"Hey! Florence! Come up stairs and see Ash!" called Violet from the doorway.

The two girls were soon seated on the bottom of the bed where Ash sat propped up by several pillows. He was begin-ning to enjoy the attention now that he was feeling more like his old self.

"You've got to stay in bed till you're recovered. Doctor Grant said you might come down for a bit this evening. But only if Mom thinks you're well enough," Violet said.

"I felt much worse than this when I had bronchitis last winter," he replied.

"That reminds me. I wonder how Albert Skinner is today," Violet mused.

At that moment, Beryl and Claire were waiting on the doorstep of Ivy Cottage for their knock to be answered. There was no sound from within so after a while Beryl knocked again, louder. Still there was no reply. Beryl tried the door

136

handle. The door was not locked. She opened the door a little and called out. She thought she heard a noise from within, and so they entered the dark house and made their way along the narrow hallway towards the door at the far end, which stood ajar.

Albert Skinner was lying face down on the floor of the small sitting room when they went in. It was so dark in there that they didn't see him at first. It was only when they heard a faint groan that they realised he was there. Beryl threw back the curtains and as daylight flooded the room, they were able to see the pitiful conditions in which the sick man existed.

A table and straight-backed chair stood on bare wooden floorboards beneath a bare light bulb suspended from the yellowing ceiling. An empty whisky bottle and a cracked cup sat side by side on the table. The walls were covered in what had once been colourful floral wallpaper that was now so stained with nicotine that the pattern was almost entirely lost. There was an overpowering smell of stale tobacco and damp in the room that made Claire feel sick. She forced a window open and took a deep breath of fresh air as Beryl turned Albert over and checked his breathing.

"Is he…?" asked Claire.

"Alive? Oh yes, he's alive. And blind drunk by the smell of his breath."

They brought him round by splashing cold water on his face and managed, with difficulty, to get him sat at the table. The fresh air blowing in through the window stirred the cigarette ash in a big glass ashtray overflowing with cigarette ends.

"You're not well, Albert. You should be in a hospital," Beryl said quietly.

"Can't go. Got to stay 'ere… Pig needs lookin' after," he wheezed.

"I know, but we can look after the pig for you till, you're well."

"Not goin' to…" he shuddered as a fit of coughing took hold of his frail body.

"Alright. Nobody's going to make you go if you don't want to. But we're not leaving unless you eat something.

We've brought you some soup. Have you got something to put it in?"

He nodded to the doorway.

Claire went hesitantly into the kitchen and shrieked as a mouse scurried across the floor into a hole in the skirting board. She pulled herself together and found a spoon and a bowl, which she carried back into the living room and filled to the brim with the delicious broth. She set it down in front of Albert and to their surprise and relief, he wolfed it down without argument.

"Don't suppose you've got a fag?" he asked as soon as he'd finished.

"How was he?" asked Violet when her mother got home.

"Awful. He did eat the soup though and we managed to get him to bed before we left."

"Let's have a cup of tea and I'll tell you all about it."

Violet was eager to know everything about Ivy Cottage. Only a few days before she would have loved nothing more than to carry out a search of the house, but things were different now. The sinister house had long been a source of speculation amongst the village children though and she just had to find out what it was really like inside.

"So, there was hardly any food in the house?" she asked when her mother had described the awful conditions she and Claire had encountered.

"Just a couple of tins of baked beans. Not even a loaf of bread or a bottle of milk. There was more pig food in the outhouse than in the kitchen. We are going to have to look after him until he can look after himself again."

"What about the pig?"

"Yes. I suppose we'll have to look after the pig as well," her mother sighed.

Chapter 22

Over the next few days, Orchard House saw the arrival of a steady stream of visitors.

Clifton and Janet Wren, Doctor Grant, Frank and Freddy, all came to see how Ash was getting on. Then one evening, Mrs Evans called in with a present.

"Just a little treat for the poor lad. Came in only yesterday," she confided, delving into the bottom of her shopping bag. A moment later, she produced a large tin of peaches.

"Oh, thank you," said Beryl. "They both love tinned fruit of any sort, but these are their favourite." As she put the tin on the kitchen table, she noticed that it was quite badly dented and there were traces of rust around the rim. "Beggars can't be choosers," she said to herself.

"How is Ashford? It must have been a terrible shock for you all. I was only saying to Mr Evans this morning… 'Stanley,' I said, it must have been a terrible shock for poor Mrs Sinton, and her not knowing where her husband is or even if he's alive.' Do you know what he said? Well no, how could you? Well, he doesn't say much as a rule, but that's because as you know he's a bit deaf and…"

"Will you stay and have a cup of tea?" Beryl asked, more to stem the flow than for any other reason.

"No, I can't stop. Thank you all the same. I've got a load of ironing to do," answered the shopkeeper. "So glad Ashford is recovering," she added as she hurried down the short path. She paused at the gate. "How is Albert, by the way? I hear you've been looking after him. I must say I don't envy you, but after all, I suppose you must feel obliged after what he did."

"We are all very grateful. It's the least we can do."

"And the Italian chap? Is he…?"

At that very moment, Ash and Salvatore came round the corner together.

"Hello Mrs Evans," said Ash politely. Salvo smiled and nodded a greeting.

The shopkeeper looked from one to the other and for once, was lost for words.

"Glad to see you out and about," she finally managed to say to Ash. "Well, I must be off." And with that, she clutched her shopping bag to her bosom and strode away.

"Look what Mrs Evans has brought you," said Beryl when Ash and Salvo went inside.

"Brilliant! Can I open them now?"

"Why don't you save them for a special occasion?" his mother replied. "And don't forget to say 'thank you' next time you go into the shop."

Ash had been up and about for a day or two by that time. He was not going to waste any more time in bed, especially during the summer holiday. Besides, he had taken on the role of pig-keeper. Albert was still too weak to do more than watch and give instructions as Ash prepared the pigswill.

A dustbin had appeared by the sty and inside it, every afternoon, Ash would find stale bread, bones, cabbage stalks, knobbly runner beans, potato peelings and all sorts of other edible scraps left by neighbours. These would all go into the pot to be boiled up and when cooled, it would be ladled out into the trough for the pig's supper. Very soon, the pig began to grow fat.

Albert did not grow fat. If anything, he grew even thinner despite the best efforts of Beryl to feed him up. He was, however, growing friendlier towards Ash, and the youngster began to see that there was more to the old chap than he had thought.

"You were in the last war, weren't you, Mr Skinner?" he ventured one evening.

Albert nodded.

"Got any medals?" Ash enquired.

"Medals? Huh!"

Ash was not sure whether this meant yes or no, but thought he probably did have.

"Can I see them?" he asked.

"Make sure the potato peelings are properly boiled," Albert replied, then shuffled off into Ivy Cottage, closing the door behind him.

Ash was careful not to bring up the subject again. Instead, their conversations were mainly about the history of the village and its inhabitants. A subject about which Albert knew a great deal having lived there all his life, like generations of Skinners before him.

Ash was becoming fond of the pig as well as its owner and decided it needed a name. 'The Pig' was too impersonal. Norman seemed like a suitable name. He somehow looked like a Norman. And so, he became Norman from then on.

Norman was adopted as The Nomad's mascot and became the most pampered pig in Sytchford. Albert would retreat indoors when other children came to feed Norman but he never once objected. Frank and Freddy carted barrow-loads of pig manure to their allotment and in return, they nailed back some of the corrugated iron that had come away from the sty roof. Norman had never had it so good.

By now, the hops were ready for picking and there was work for the whole village in the various farms along the valley. The workforce was traditionally boosted by women and children from the industrial towns, but this year, there were fewer than usual as so many women were employed, like Claire, in the armaments industry. To make up for this shortage, all the schoolchildren were recruited into the fields. Every morning, Salvatore would pick them up from the crossroads with the tractor and trailer and take them to wherever they were needed while Claire was collected by a bus ferrying worker to the munitions factory at Baggots Wood.

Ash and Violet were recruited for the harvest, and so one morning, they joined thirty others, all carrying flasks of tea and brown paper packages containing sandwiches to see them through the day. The children were aged from about nine to fourteen and a few mothers accompanied younger ones as well. There was an atmosphere of excitement amongst the children as they waited to be collected; almost as though they were on an outing to the seaside, and when Salvatore arrived, a cheer went up. They clambered aboard the trailer and sat on bales of straw, packed together tightly, glad of the warmth of the bodies next to them in the early morning chill. Rain had fallen overnight and showers of muddy water splattered the verges as the tractor wheels churned through the deep ruts and puddles along the lane. The rain clouds were drifting away however, and the sun was breaking through, promising a fine day.

Florence was already at work when the trailer turned into the hop field. The other Nomads went to join her and she showed them what to do. The work wasn't hard really. First, the hop bines had to be pulled down from the wires, which they had spent all summer winding around.

Then the hops had to be picked off and thrown into baskets, which were weighed and then emptied into a trailer. When the trailer was full, off it would go to the kilns, where the hops would be dried.

Every picker kept a tally of how many baskets they had managed to fill, and that would determine how much they got paid. Ash and Violet, like all the other kids, would hand over their earnings to their mother and she would give them some pocket money to buy treats. What she kept would go on new clothes for her children who were rapidly outgrowing all their old things.

Soon, the friends had sorted out an efficient system which allowed them to fill the baskets quickly. Frank and Freddy pulled the hops down while the other three stripped the hops off. They worked till 10 'o'clock and then stopped for a breakfast cup of tea. Midday, they had a short lunch break and at four o'clock, the children climbed back on board the trailer to go home. Gradually, one by one, the hop fields were harvested.

One day, when the harvest was nearly over, The Nomads slipped away through a hole in the hedge during their lunch break. They had come to the orchard looking for the early Worcester apples that were now ready to eat. Ash filled a bag with bruised windfalls as a treat for Norman then joined the others sitting in the shade of the trees munching apples.

"Won't be long before the harvest's finished," Florence said.

"Then we'll start on the apple orchards," said Ash.

"We won't be here then," she said sadly.

"Why?" asked Ash with surprise.

"We're leaving soon," she replied.

"Why? Where to? When?" the others all asked at once.

"Listen, it's like this," Florence said, twisting at a blade of grass around her fingers. "I've just had a letter from my ma saying how much she misses me. She wants me to go back to live with her in Kent."

"But what about your grandparents? Don't they need you to be with them?" asked Violet as she knelt in front of her friend.

Florence sighed and shook her head.

"They'll be alright. After they drop me off at Worcester to catch the train, they're going on to meet up with Gran's family over Evesham way. I'm going to miss them though."

"Are you coming back?" asked Ash.

Florence shrugged.

"I hope so."

The children were unusually subdued when they returned to their work in the hop fields that afternoon.

Soon, the last of the hop fields was stripped bare and swallows gathered in chattering flocks on fences and telegraph wires, preparing to fly south for the winter. At the Gypsy campsite, the Lovesmith family was busy preparing for their own journey. One day, Granddad and Alf jacked the vardo up and removed the wheels to grease the wheel axles. A few of the wheel-spokes were found to be riddled with woodworm, and so they had to be taken out and replaced with new ones. Work that would delay their departure by a couple of weeks.

"Better to find it now than when we were on the road," Granddad observed glumly as he and Alf rolled the wheel into the smithy.

By mid-September, the summer holidays were over and Ash and Violet were back in school every day. The Turner twins went as often as they could. Florence was busy either on the farm or helping get the caravan ready for the journey, so the friends had little time to spend together.

One Saturday afternoon, Ash and Violet were on their way down Whispering Lane to feed Norman when they saw the corpulent figure of Dr Grant coming out of Ivy Cottage.

"Hello, doctor. How is Mr Skinner today?" asked Violet.

"I'm afraid he's not at all well," replied the doctor. "In fact, I have telephoned for an ambulance to take him to the infirmary."

"What's the matter with him?" asked Ash

"Pneumonia, I fear," the doctor answered. "Ah, here comes the ambulance now."

The children watched silently as the vehicle reversed carefully down the narrow lane.

"He's through here," said the doctor as he led the way followed by the ambulance crew. Ash stepped aside to give both women more room as they manoeuvred a stretcher through the gateway. After a few minutes, they emerged from the house with Albert on the stretcher covered in blankets. He seemed unconscious, but as he was carried past the children, he raised his head slightly and managed to whisper, "Feed pig."

"We'll look after him. Don't worry," said Ash as the stretcher was loaded into the ambulance.

As the vehicle drove away watched by a handful of villagers, Violet and Ash crossed their fingers behind their backs as they always did when they saw an ambulance.

"I'm going to be an ambulance driver one day," Violet said to her mother that evening.

"Are you?" Beryl said. "What made you decide that?"

"Just seeing those two women fetch Albert away. I never knew that women could be ambulance drivers."

Later, when Violet was about to climb the stairs to go to bed, she turned to her mother.

"Will he come back, do you think?"

"Who? Oh Albert, you mean? I don't know."

"You thought I meant Dad."

"Your dad *will* come back. Granny Lovesmith said so."

"You don't believe in fortune telling," replied Violet.

"Well, perhaps I do… sometimes," her mother conceded with a smile.

Chapter 23

Albert Skinner's funeral was held at midday one Friday in late September.

The church bell that had been tolling for an hour fell silent and even the rooks in the rookery stopped squabbling as Clifton Wren greeted the mourners at the church door.

The Sintons took their places in a pew close to the front. Fresh hops had been hung along the rails on either side of the aisle; not in honour of the deceased, but in preparation for the harvest festival service next week.

They sat just behind Mrs Evans and Mrs Little, who talked non-stop commenting on what others were wearing as though they were at a fashion show. Four men carried Albert Skinner's coffin up the aisle: Joe Leonard, Salvatore, Reg Tolley and Alf Carter. They put down their burden in front of the altar and took their places in the front pews. Looking round, Ash saw a few other villagers scattered about, but most of the pews remained empty, and the combined voices of the congregation were drowned out by the church organ as they sang the first hymn: 'Jerusalem'.

The funeral service followed the traditional lines that Clifton Wren knew only too well and he might have been forgiven for treating this one as routine. Routine was not the way however, that the vicar would ever treat such an event. As far as he was concerned, no departing soul deserved anything less than the best farewell he could offer. And so, his voice was the one heard singing most enthusiastically. It did help somewhat that he had chosen some of his most favourite hymns and 'Jerusalem' always got things off to a good start, in his opinion.

Joseph Leonard then stood up and spoke of Albert's bravery in the First World War and the all lives he had saved. He went on to praise his service to the community as Air Raid Warden in the current conflict.

The vicar spoke about how Albert had saved Ash's life. A deed that, he said, would always be remembered in the village.

At this point Beryl Sinton noticed tears streaming down Violet's cheeks.

"Don't be sad Violet. He's gone to a much better place," she whispered, squeezing her daughter's hand.

The short service concluded with The Lord's Prayer and the congregation filed out to gather at the graveside.

Amongst the little group dressed in grey and black, there was only one scrap of colour; the bunch of dahlias Beryl had picked from her garden to lay on the coffin. A few leaves floated by on the freshening breeze as the coffin was lowered to its resting place, watched from a discreet distance by Sam Turner waiting with a shovel in his hand.

In the Crystal Ball lounge, the tables had been laid ready for the wake. To everyone's surprise, Albert had left a sum of money with the landlord to provide for a proper send-off. There were plates of sandwiches containing ham, cheese, egg and corned beef. Beryl had baked a raspberry jam sponge cake and Mrs Evans had supplied a large tinned fruit jelly. Teapots stood ready for action and for the children, there were bottles of dandelion and burdock lemonade. More food was assembled there than anyone had seen in one place since rationing began.

It wasn't long after the meal got underway that Violet noticed how many more villagers seemed to be there than had been at the church; Mr Evans for one. He had sneaked in carrying a pint of beer from the bar. Violet was particularly angry about that. In all the time she had been keeping watch on Ivy Cottage, she recalled he was the only visitor. On several occasions, she had seen them going to the pub together, and yet he couldn't be bothered to go to the funeral of his pal. She gave him one of her most withering looks as he helped himself to the sandwiches.

"I'm surprised Albert had the money for this sort of spread," said Claire.

"He wasn't short of money. He just didn't like to part with it… when he was alive," replied Beryl.

"So, he didn't need to live the way he did?" mumbled Ash.

"Don't speak with your mouth full. How many times have I told you about that?" his mother responded.

Soon, the room began to fill with cigarette smoke. Most people seemed not to notice, but Mrs Evans was annoyed and Claire overheard her complaining about it to Mrs Little.

"I mean to say! Why don't they ration cigarettes and alcohol, the same as everything else? All this smoke can't be good for a person!"

"I know," agreed her friend. "If you ask me, they ought to get one of them distractor fans."

When Violet and Ash couldn't eat any more, they were sent outside to get some fresh air. They sat on one of the wooden benches with their backs against the pub wall from where they could see all along the high street and beyond the crossroads towards the Gypsy campsite. They were hoping for some military vehicles to come along, but the roads were empty and deserted as usual.

A black cat casually strolled across the road and jumped up besides Violet, purring softly as she stroked it. Soon, it curled up and settled down to sleep. It was a familiar sight to everyone in the village, although no one knew who owned it. It came and went as it pleased and always seemed to be well-fed. Violet had tried to make it her own once. She fed it every day for a week and one evening, shut it in the wash house. Next morning, when she opened the door, the cat had dashed off and wasn't seen for weeks afterwards.

"It's so sad, isn't it?" said Violet. "Practically starving to death when there's no need. I wonder why he lived like that."

"I dunno. What's going to happen to Norman? That's what I'm wondering."

"Listen, Ash. Never mind the pig. Our dad might be hungry somewhere. He could be starving. I've read in the papers how prisoners of war are treated in some places. It doesn't

148

make sense going hungry when there's no need!" she continued.

"Look! It's Florence!" said Ash as he spotted a horse-drawn caravan approaching. They ran to meet them at the crossroads.

"You're leaving!" said Ash. "Why didn't you say?"

"I called this morning, but there was no one there."

"You must have missed us. We've been to the funeral" Violet explained.

"I'm sorry I couldn't be there. I wrote you a letter," she pulled out an envelope and handed it to Ash. "I was going to put it through your letterbox if you weren't there when we went past."

"Why have you got to go?" asked Violet.

"We're travellers. It's what we do. We'll be back."

"Promise?"

"Promise."

"Wait. I've got something for you," said Ash as he dashed off towards home.

He emerged soon after, carrying something roughly wrapped in brown paper.

"What is it?" asked Florence as he handed it to her.

"Something you'll like. Open it when you make camp this evening."

"Bye," called Granddad and Granny Lovesmith as they geed-up Nelson and set off.

Ash and Violet watched as the caravan rolled past the Crystal Ball. The black cat opened its eyes as they passed, yawned and went back to sleep.

"Say goodbye to Frank and Freddy for me," Florence called back. "See you next year."

"Write!" shouted Ash.

"I will!" came the faint reply.

When the caravan disappeared from sight over the bridge, the roads seemed even emptier than they had before, and it was with heavy hearts that the two children returned to sit by the cat.

From within the pub, the sounds of revelry grew steadily louder. Someone began to play the piano, and voices were raised, singing along to some of the popular tunes. When it came, as it always did, to 'We'll meet again', Violet could stand it no longer. She went home leaving Ash where he was hoping someone would remember and take him a glass of lemonade.

That evening, the Sinton household was unusually quiet as they sat around the kitchen table reflecting on the day's events. Even the good news on the wireless did little to lighten the mood. Allied advances were gathering pace and with Russian troops making headway from the east, the war was surely coming to an end before much longer.

Violet felt tired. Ash felt miserable. Beryl and Claire were both wearied by the on-going hardships and by the long struggle to maintain hope.

"Get the chip pan out, Claire. Let's have some supper," said Beryl, and suddenly things seemed better all round.

"I forgot to tell you what Mrs Little said this afternoon," Claire began as she put the chip pan on the range. "Well, Mrs Evans was complaining about the cigarette smoke and…"

Things in the Evans household were not so good though. Mr Evans was nursing a painfully bruised knee. He had tripped on the doorstep leaving the pub and fallen awkwardly, much to Mrs Evans' embarrassment. Now to add to his injury, he was being lectured on his drinking habits by his wife. He had "shown her up in public" and for that, he would have to suffer.

The Lovesmiths had made camp by the roadside some distance from Sytchford. Their journey had been uneventful on the deserted road, and they sat under the stars, savouring bowls of rabbit stew.

"I've got a surprise for us," said Florence when they finished mopping their bowls with chunks of crusty bread. She got to her feet and disappeared into the caravan. Moments later, she reappeared in the firelight holding out a dented tin of peaches.

"They were a present from Ash," she said. "Wonder what they taste like."

"Only one way to find out. Where's the tin opener?" said Granddad.

Next morning, Violet and Claire were out in the garden, clearing away the leaves that had come down overnight covering the lawn.

"I've got something I need to tell you," Violet said.

"I'm sorry," she began as she sat on the garden swing with her head down. "I know I shouldn't have spied on you like I did, but I didn't do it on purpose."

"Well, it's a good job you and Florence were following me or things would have not turned out as well as they did. Budge up. Let me have a seat," Claire replied as she squeezed into the gap Violet made. "How did you find out about us anyway?"

"That's another thing," Violet sighed. "I want to apologise to Mr Skinner, but it's too late."

"Apologise for what?"

"For spying on him. That's what I was doing when I saw you and Salvo by Cooper's Mill. I was watching through Ash's binoculars from up at the rock house."

"Why were you spying on Albert Skinner?" Claire asked. "What did he have to do with anything?"

"We thought he and Mr Evans were selling food on the black market, and I wanted to get evidence so that it could be stopped. I don't know anymore. Perhaps I was wrong," she added, looking at her sister.

"What made you think that, Violet?"

"Well one day, we found a whole load of tinned food hidden in an old barn and..."

"When was this?" Her sister interrupted.

"Remember when there was that big thunderstorm?"

"That was the day Florence arrived, wasn't it?"

"That's right. Well, it was the day after."

"And this hoard of tinned food was in the old barn in Lower Meadow?"

"Yes. How did you know?" said Violet, taken by surprise.

"Because I heard Mr Leonard and Mr Evans talking about it one day. Mr Evans' storeroom needed to have the roof repaired, and while that was being, done Mr Leonard let him use the barn to store his stock. He wasn't hiding anything. It was all above board."

"Oh no," cried Violet. "How could I be so stupid? You won't tell Mom, will you? I feel so ashamed of myself," she added, blushing in embarrassment.

"There's no need to feel like that. You were doing what you thought was best," her sister replied.

"But I was wrong," Violet insisted.

"Listen. When things are going badly people always look for someone to blame. That's just human nature I'm afraid. The important thing is to learn from our mistakes, and you have learned, haven't you?"

Violet just nodded and gave her sister a hug.

"Is there anything else you want to tell me?" Claire added.

"No. I don't think so."

"It wasn't you who wrote the anonymous letter then?"

"No. I couldn't do something like that."

"I didn't think it was you, but I had to be sure."

"Somebody wrote it though. I wonder who it was," Violet said.

"Anyway, it doesn't really matter now, does it?" Claire replied. "But from now on let's not keep secrets from one another. There's been too many of those lately."

"No. No more secrets," Violet agreed.

Beryl watched from the kitchen window as Claire pushed Violet higher and higher on the swing as the sound of laughter rang out across the garden.

Chapter 24

Not long afterwards, on a bright, frosty morning, Ash and Violet met Frank and Freddy and they wandered aimlessly towards the smithy. The campsite was, of course, deserted, but seeing it somehow made Florence's absence a reality.

"What shall we do?" asked Ash as he listlessly kicked an empty tin can into the brambles.

"How about going to Avens Wood?" suggested Freddy.

"Yeah! It's about time The Nomads went back to the rock house," said Frank.

"There's some big horse chestnut trees in the wood. We can get some conkers," added Freddy.

"I'll get my binoculars on the way," said Ash.

Before long, they were climbing the steep winding track that led to the rock house. It had become overgrown in places with nettles and tall willow-herbs all gone to seed. They had to cut a path through with hazel switches to reach their old HQ.

Clearly, no one had been there for weeks, and everything was just as it had been except that the elder branches were now weighed down with bunches of purple-black berries and the leaves on the trees were no longer the fresh green of spring and summer. They now looked tired and dusty and any day now, they would turn to their autumn yellows, browns and reds.

They sat on the bench outside the rock house, watching the noisy jays flying backwards and forwards collecting acorns to bury for their winter larders. The landscape looked different now that the hops had all been stripped exposing a skeleton of poles and wires across the fields. The orchard trees were dotted with red apples and the hedgerows had grown big and bushy.

Violet took the binoculars from where they lay on the bench and climbed to the lookout rock. From where she stood, the houses in Sytchford looked no bigger than tiny matchboxes. She put the binoculars to her eyes and found Orchard House. Her mother was just leaving the front door with a shopping bag over her arm. Violet felt uncomfortable watching her mother. It seemed as though she was, somehow, spying on her, but of course, she wasn't.

She swung the binoculars away and saw that the bus was crossing the bridge heading towards the crossroads. She focused and followed it to where it stopped outside the Crystal Ball. Several people got off. Violet recognised all of them except one man in RAF uniform. He walked with the aid of a walking stick towards the crossroads. He looked familiar. She swung back to Orchard House. Her mother had dropped the shopping bag and was running.

Violet called, "Ash! Come here! Quick!" as she watched her father and mother throw their arms around each other.

They ran all the way home without stopping and arrived hot, sweaty and out of breath. They tumbled through the kitchen door and stopped dead in their tracks when they saw their father. He was so much thinner than he had been when they last saw him, but it was the livid scar running down the left-hand side of his face, that shocked them most. For a moment they gaped speechless, then he opened his arms and they ran towards him feeling only joy and happiness at being reunited. And that evening he told them how it was that he had survived.

"We were flying over the mountains on a reconnaissance mission behind enemy lines," he began. "We ran into anti-aircraft gunfire and must have been hit because one engine suddenly caught fire and we started to spin out of control. We knew we were going to crash. The plane was filling with smoke and spiralling down. Somehow, I managed to bail out. That's how I got this," he pointed to the scar. "And the broken leg. I survived, but the pilot wasn't so lucky. Anyway, I came down in an olive grove on a hillside close to a little village. The parachute caught in one of the trees and I was left hanging in mid-air. The plane crash must have alerted everyone for miles around and I was expecting to be taken prisoner – or shot. I was lucky though, because the villagers were partisans waging guerrilla war against the Nazis. They got to me first and hid me. They had next to nothing, but what little food they had, they shared with me. I was moved about from place to place. Caves, shepherd's huts, abandoned ruins, anywhere they could find to keep me safe. They would have been shot if I was ever discovered. They risked their lives for my sake. Eventually, they managed to smuggle me over the front line into allied territory and I was eventually put on a ship home. So here I am. I can hardly believe it."

Ash and Violet had a thousand questions to ask: How did they treat his broken leg? What did he eat? Were there wild boar and bears in the mountains?

Eventually, he held his hands up and said, "Wait a minute. One at a time. I'll tell you all about it, but first tell me what's been happening at home while I've been away."

It was late that evening when the excited children were finally persuaded to go to bed, and they were up early the next morning hardly daring to believe that their father had really returned.

"I thought it might have been a dream," said Violet as she sat opposite him at breakfast.

In the next few days, the Sinton family settled down happily and resumed life with a renewed sense of hope for the future. Sidney began to regain his health and Claire announced that as soon as the war was over, she would train to become a teacher. Violet and Ash began collecting fallen leaves and branches to build a bonfire for Guy Fawkes Night.

Norman's future was hanging in the balance. The village butcher had, on more than one occasion, tried to buy him from Albert and hoped that he might now manage to acquire the animal from the deceased man's estate.

Norman was woken early one frosty morning by the sound of the tractor and small, covered trailer as they approached the pigsty.

The tractor came to a stop and a man climbed down. He walked to the back of the trailer and dropped the tailgate with a loud clang. The pig instinctively backed away into the furthest corner of the pen sensing danger as the man opened the gate. Then he heard a familiar voice.

"Come on, Norman. It's only me. Look what I've got for you."

Ash appeared carrying a bucket full of steaming mash which wafted a delicious smell across the pigsty. Norman was still wary of the stranger, but he was also hungry. Ash coaxed the pig to the gate. The stranger had backed off some way down the lane and Norman felt a little more comfortable. He had spent his whole life in the pigsty though and was reluctant to venture outside. Ash produced an apple from his pocket and dropped it on the ground. That was too much for Norman to refuse and he stepped into the lane and gobbled up the offering greedily. Bit by bit, Ash coaxed the pig up the ramp and into the trailer. Norman had his snout deep in the bucket when he heard the tailgate bang shut behind him.

"Well done, lad," said Joseph Leonard. "You handled that very well."

"What will happen to him now?" asked Violet when Ash returned to Orchard House for his breakfast.

"Mr Leonard is keeping him to breed from. He reckons he's the best Gloucester Old Spot boar he's ever seen. There aren't many left and he says that if somebody doesn't do something about it soon, the breed will die out altogether."

"So, that pig's got an important role to play by the sound of it," said their mother as she loaded a toast rack and brought it to the table.

"Mr Leonard said I can go and visit him whenever I like. He said I'd make a good stockman when I grow up," Ash said proudly.

"Is that what you'd like to do when you leave school?" asked his father, putting down his teacup.

"Yes, either that or an explorer," he replied.

"I'm going to be a vet," said Violet.

"I thought you were going to be an ambulance driver," laughed Claire.

"Well, yes I was, but I've changed my mind."

"*Again,*" scoffed Ash.

"That's alright. Violet can change her mind if she wants to," said their mother. "You've both got all the time in the world to decide what you're going to become."

"I think I just heard the postman," said Claire as she went to the front door.

Sure enough, there was a letter lying on the mat. She picked it up and looked at it with surprise before she returned to the kitchen and put it down on the table in front of Ash.

"It's for you," she said.

The room fell silent as they all looked at the long brown envelope. It had a cellophane window through which they could see a neatly typed address.

"Aren't you going to open it?" asked his father as Ash sat staring at with an expression of deep mistrust. He had seen envelopes of this type before and they usually meant trouble of one sort or another. He picked it up and, taking a deep breath, he slipped a finger under the corner of the flap and tore it open. The letter read as follows:

As executor for the last will and testimony of Mr Albert Skinner, late of Ivy Cottage, Whispering Cottage, Whispering Lane, Sytchford, we are pleased to inform you that he has bequeathed you his First World War medals, in recognition of your, and your family's help and assistance. These items are in our safekeeping and can be collected at your convenience. Alternatively, we would be pleased to deliver them to you for a small remuneration.

We await your further instructions.
Doddermore and Godfrey,
Solicitors.

"He left me his medals!" Ash gasped. "At least I think that's what it means."

"Let me see," said his mother.

Ash handed her the piece of paper and she read the contents out loud. When she came to the end, she sat down with a hand over her mouth. Her eyes were swimming in tears.

"What's the matter? It's good, isn't it?" Violet asked, looking puzzled.

"Yes... yes, of course. It's very good," she replied. "I'm sorry. I don't know what came over me."

She blew her nose and smiled with a little dismissive wave of her hand.

"When can we go and collect them?" Ash wanted to know.

"Best make an appointment. I'll phone them later," his mother suggested.

"Let's clear the table. There's something I want you to see."

When the table was clear, she fetched the photo album and they all sat down again.

Together, they turned the pages. Behind every picture was a story, a memory. There were only a few of the children's grandparents and just two of their great-grandparents, and they were all the more precious because of this.

They came to a page where three soldiers were pictured outside the Crystal Ball. Beryl's father stood between a young Joseph Leonard and Albert Skinner. All three were smiling happily and holding glasses of beer, clearly enjoying themselves.

"They look so young, don't they?" Sidney said.

Someone had written their names below the photograph, and the date, 1914.

That afternoon, the black cat jumped down off the garden fence and trotted across the lawn and through the flower border to the back door. It sat there and began to lick clean its paws and whiskers.

Since the old man with the pig had disappeared, it had missed the food that was always waiting for it on the doorstep of the house. It had called as usual for a while, until it sensed that the man was gone for good. So now it was time to find someone else willing to provide a regular saucer of milk or a few scraps during the coming winter. Perhaps the girl who had fed it so well for a while last winter might do so again, so long as it didn't mean going into the little house where it had been trapped one night. It would wait patiently. Sooner or later, the door would open and who knew what would happen then?

THE END